TO DUST RETURN

MICHAEL NEWTON

WOLFPACK
PUBLISHING
— EST 2013 —

**WOLFPACK
PUBLISHING**
— EST 2013 —

Published in the United States by Wolfpack Publishing, Las Vegas

Wolfpack Publishing
6032 Wheat Penny Avenue
Las Vegas, NV 89122

wolfpackpublishing.com

Paperback ISBN 978-1-64734-906-6
eBook ISBN 978-1-64734-905-9

TO DUST RETURN

"In the sweat of thy face shalt thou eat bread, till thou return unto the ground; for out of it wast thou taken: for dust thou art, and unto dust shalt thou return."

Genesis 3:19, King James Version

"It is from the Bible that man has learned cruelty, rapine, and murder; for the belief of a cruel God makes a cruel man."

Thomas Paine, *The Age of Reason*

For Josh and Joe

1

Lyon County, Kansas

A preacher with a harsh, cracked voice, verging on laryngitic, shouted from the stolen Studebaker's dashboard radio, calling for *Jaysus-uh* to smite the land and all its unbelievers for abandoning their faith of old and chasing after wicked Socialism, led by Franklin Roosevelt.

"Too late," the driver answered back, gray eyes sweeping a landscape well and truly smitten to the point of death.

He gripped the steering wheel lightly, one-handed, marveling at how much motor vehicles had changed in recent years. It was a miracle of sorts, considering how few Americans could still afford to buy new models in the midst of a depression, with one-quarter of the nation's people jobless, thousands of them rolling aimlessly across the continent like tumbleweeds, in search of nonexistent work.

Most of that exodus was westward bound these days, pursuing a mirage of hope somewhere beyond the Rockies, caravans of last-gasp trucks and flivvers packed with useless things the pilgrims couldn't bear to leave behind, hobos willing to risk a beating or their lives to stow away in empty railroad cars. Some tributaries of that human flood were sidetracked into major cities, praying for a part-time job or handout, mostly winding up in dead-end shantytowns.

Only the shouting preacher and his brethren, fading in and out across the dial, seemed conscious of the fact that humankind had brought this down upon itself.

The driver could have told them that.

Instead, he leaned toward object lessons in the flesh.

Holding the Studebaker—their Commander model, made in South Bend, Indiana, with six cylinders growling beneath its hood—at sixty miles per hour, the auto thief, least of his sins, reached out and spun the Motorola's knob, muting the preacher in mid-shout, scrolling through static till he hit upon Bing Crosby crooning his big hit from two years back, "Sweet Georgia Brown."

It's been said she knocks 'em dead when she lands in town.

Prophetic words. And Georgia Brown wasn't alone.

A dying farm heaved into view a quarter-hour later, offset to the rural highway's eastern side. The driver slowed and scanned it, the ramshackle house, once proud, wind-blasted now; a swaybacked barn; empty corral and sheds that looked as if another storm might take them down; a one-hole privy situated well off from the house, to spare the outdoor well.

It seemed deserted at first glance, but then the driver saw a thin, stoop-shouldered man in overalls, wearing a slouch hat, working through his list of daily chores that wouldn't help a thing unless the blue sky clouded over and began to rain at last.

"Don't hold your breath," the car thief muttered, as he silenced Crosby on the radio.

He slowed and turned into a dirt driveway, coasting along until be stopped a hundred feet out from the house. The farmer, watching him approach, didn't appear to have a weapon on him, but in times like these you couldn't be too careful.

Switching off the Studebaker's Big Six engine, the intruder reached across and took a dogeared copy of the Holy Bible from the seat beside him. Pasting on a smile, aware that some folks deemed him handsome in a way he'd never understood, the driver stepped out of his stolen ride and started ambling toward the house. Somewhere beyond it, younger voices, audible but indistinct, told him the family was all at home.

He kept the greeting cheery. "Mr. Halliday, I don't know whether you remember me?"

"I know you," said the farmer.

"Excellent. It's been a while."

"Three months or so, as I recall."

"That's right."

"You've got a better car this time."

"I made an advantageous trade."

"What can I help you with?" the farmer asked, not really meaning it. He would have precious little help to offer anyone, and even less desire to dole it out for strangers.

"Other way around," his uninvited two-time visitor replied. He held the Bible with its cover toward the sodbuster. "I'm sharing the good news with anyone who needs some."

"Preaching," said the farmer. He was in his early forties but looked ten years older, leeched of hope. His dark eyes would have seen it all by now, expecting no more from the future than another sucker punch. "There's nothing for you here, Parson. We barely get by as it is."

We. A father, mother, and two children.

"Just a moment of your time, perhaps?" The interloper glanced around, showing he understood the farmer might have time to spare, even if it was running out. "To share His word of hope?"

"No thanks, unless you've got a prayer to conjure rain."

"I couldn't promise that, sir."

"Didn't think so. Now, if you'll excuse me…"

A dismissal, brooking no refusal.

"As you wish, sir." Half turned toward his vehicle, the visitor glimpsed movement from the farmhouse, saw a woman watching from its open doorway.

Perfect.

Back behind the Studebaker's wheel, he turned around, raising a plume of dust, and started back toward the highway. Flat land meant he would have to drive a mile or two before the farm was out of sight, but he had time to kill.

*　*　*

"Who was that, Pa?"

Thaddeus Halliday, just turned eleven, watched the car receding, turning north onto the state highway.

"Nobody," Aaron told his son. Added, "A preacher with his hand out."

"Spent some money on that Studie, though," Tad said.

"The question is *whose* money?"

Stepping up behind her brother, Rose of Sharon said, "Come on, Tad. Barn won't clean itself."

"Cleaned it last week," the boy reminded her.

"And now it's *this* week," she replied. "Nothing stays done

4

around a farm."

Tad thought of something smart to answer back, about how all the livestock left to them were chickens now, and they were disappearing into stew, no more than half a dozen left to go and barely making any mess inside the clapped-out barn, before their father cut him off.

"Do like your sister says, now."

"Yes, sir."

Thinking to himself as he trailed Rose of Sharon toward the barn, *I'd love to see inside that Studebaker, though. Imagine that.*

***

The car thief found an access road that seemed to lead no-where and turned in, drove a hundred yards off from the pavement, walking speed, keeping the Studebaker's dust trail to a minimum.

He doubted that the farmer would be watching, glad to see the back of him, but there were kids around the place, and he had sensed a wariness about the woman peering at him from her front door, cautious around strangers who had no reason for dropping by.

The driver stopped, set the Commander's parking brake although it couldn't roll away and leave him stranded on flatland. He got out, stretched, and walked around behind the car to pop its trunk.

Time to prepare.

He had a ritual and never deviated from it, stripping down to long johns, neatly laying out his slacks, coat, tie and dress shirt on the car's backseat before he suited up for battle in familiar olive drab.

The tunic first, then trousers with their light blue piping designating infantry. Russet brown combat boots came next, laced snuggly to the top, then puttees wrapped around the boots and lower calves like bandages. Atop all that, an overcoat whose hem reached to his knees.

Around his narrow waist, a belt secured the overcoat. On his right hip, an M1911 semiautomatic pistol nestled in a flap holster, its magazine loaded with seven .45 ACP rounds, plus one more in the chamber. Pouches for spare magazines rode on each side of the belt's polished buckle.

On the soldier's left hip, sheathed, a Mark I trench knife balanced out the load. Its knuckleduster handle, forged from bronze and chemically blackened, had cast spikes on the bow of each knuckle. A conical steel nut held the knife's blade in place, doubling as a tool for cracking skulls. The seven-inch blade, blued with a black oxide finish to prevent it from reflecting moonlight, was double-edged for thrusting and slashing, honed to a fine razor's edge.

Before donning his M1917 helmet, nearly half a million purchased from the Brits on U.S. entry to the Great War, nicknamed *Salatschüssel*—"salad bowl"—by warriors of the other side, he drew a French-made M2 gas mask from its canvas case and pulled the straps over his slicked-back hair, adjusting them until the mask covered his whole face from the hairline to his chin. It was designed to shield the wearer from at least five hours' exposure to mustard or phosgene gas but now served mainly to conceal this warrior's face from witnesses.

Not that he planned on leaving anyone alive.

The next-to-last step was extracting two small cotton

wool balls from a pocket of his overcoat and wedging them into his ears.

And finally, he took his rifle from its leather case. It was an M1917 Enfield, measuring forty-six inches overall, with a twenty-six-inch barrel, tipping the scale at 9.2 pounds with its six-round magazine empty. Chambered for .30-06 Springfield cartridges, it held six in the mag and fired from a modified Mauser turn bolt, but for some unknown reason clips used for reloading held only five shells. Its .30-caliber M2 Ball projectiles weighed eleven grams apiece and left the Enfield's muzzle at 2,800 feet per second, delivering 2,820 foot-pounds of destructive energy at the rifle's effective firing range of six hundred yards. A lucky shot might kill or maim at nine times that distance, but that was wishful thinking over open sights.

The Enfield's capper was an M1917 sword bayonet, featuring a seventeen-inch fluted, spear-point blade, designed to transfix an opponent in close-quarters combat, capable of pinning two together if the opportunity arose.

Prepared at last, breath rasping through the gas mask, he began the walk back to the farm he'd chosen for his latest sacrifice.

The barren, wind-scourged fields reminded him of no man's land, an image from another life and half a world away.

***

Rose Halliday disliked her full first name and never used it unless legally compelled to do so, as when signing up for school. She knew her parents took it from the Bible, in the Song of Solomon, but personally saw it as old-fashioned and inviting mockery.

Rose's paternal grandparents had named her father Aaron, after the prophet and brother of Moses, barred from Canaan with his sibling for their mutual impatience. That fit Aaron Halliday, at least, a quality that had defined much of his life and only worsened as he watched relentless nature steal away what he had built up for his family.

Rose's mother, Naomi, bore another biblical name, but hers had a bright side, translated from Hebrew to English as pleasant, lovely, or winsome. All had been appropriate at one time or another until the Depression struck and drought supplied the coup de gras to hopeful dreams. Today, Naomi Halliday was ghostlike, fading, although still devoted to her family.

And Rose's brother, Thaddeus, had not escaped, named for the least known among Christ's apostles in the Gospels, said to mean "courageous heart," although some preachers mixed him up with Judas the betrayer.

Little brothers could be like that, Rose had learned.

"You see that car, Rose?" Thad was asking her as they approached the barn.

"I didn't notice it," she lied.

"How could you *not*? Just think of cruising in that thing, no chores to do, heading for anyplace at all."

"That's not real life," she answered back.

"Seems like it is for him."

"Maybe you ought to be a preacher, then. Start memorizing scripture now, you should be ready by the time you're… what? Forty? Fifty?"

Glancing at her brother's empty hands, she asked, "You have the toolbox?"

Thad stopped short, cheeks coloring. "Goldarn it!" Turning toward the house, he chirped, "Be right back."

"Don't stall, telling Ma about that car. She saw it for herself."

"Yeah, yeah."

Rose went inside the barn, remembering when there'd been milk cows in its stalls and bales of hay piled in the loft. Today, it only sheltered dust, some of its boards hanging askew where nails had rusted out and lost their hold on aged wood.

She saw Thad's point about the daily jobs assigned to them, but what else could a body do, beyond small daily bids to hold the line against an enemy no man could hope to vanquish?

From the yard, she heard her father's voice, calling, "Naomi, fetch my twelve."

Meaning his twelve-gauge lever-action shotgun, made by Winchester, their Model 1887, holding five rounds in its magazine beneath its thirty-inch barrel, a weapon you could use for hunting small game or for self-defense.

What was he thinking, calling for it in the middle of the day?

Rose turned back toward the barnyard, lingering in shadow as she peered out into sunlight and beheld a solitary figure trudging toward the house across a onetime cornfield, wasteland now.

They had no neighbors within easy walking distance since the last round of dust storms, and Rose had no idea who this could be, unless…

The moving form looked *wrong* somehow, its head distorted, while the long coat had to be uncomfortable in the morning's heat. And what was that the stranger carried? Long and slender, like a gun.

"Papa!" she called out to her father.

He was nearly halfway to the porch now, saying, "Hurry

9

up!" as Ma emerged, the shotgun in her hands.

Rose of Sharon glanced back at the figure in their field and found it standing stock-still now, aiming. She saw a distant puff of smoke and flinched involuntarily, a half-second before the *crack* of gunfire reached her ears.

***

The Enfield bucked against its owner's shoulder. He absorbed the long-familiar recoil, thankful for the cotton in his ears that robbed the gunshot's echo of its lancing sting.

Down range, he saw the bullet strike its target with a cloud of dust tinged crimson, punch the farmer through a single stutter-step before he dropped facedown into the dusty yard. Chickens scattered away from him, running for cover on the far side of the porch.

Wifey recoiled and nearly dropped the weapon she was carrying, too slow to arm her man in self-defense. She sobbed a name, but it was lost to distance, didn't reach the marksman's ears. He worked the Enfield's bolt, the spent brass arcing out of sight before he sighted down and fired a second time, punching the woman backward through the open doorway where she'd stood to watch him earlier.

Two down.

The soldier cycled out another empty cartridge, stooping to retrieve both from the dry earth to his right and pocket them. He straightened as a small boy ran up to the farmhouse shouting for his parents, neither of them likely to respond. Taking his time, the soldier paced off twenty feet or so, watching the boy kneel at his supine mother's side.

Farm boys grew up with death but losing someone that

you knew and cared about was different from watching live-stock slaughtered for a meal.

Or should be, anyway.

The sniper found his mark, allowing for the eighteen ounces that his bayonet added, protruding from the Enfield's muzzle. Squeezing off his third round within ninety seconds, give or take, he saw the boy collapse across his mother's body with the shotgun trapped between them.

Good enough, so far.

But there had been *two* voices audible behind the farmhouse while he passed time with the dwindling family's patriarch. Which meant one target still alive and likely on the run.

From what he'd heard before, the soldier figured it must be a girl.

And that would make his day, with any luck extending well past nightfall.

***

Rose of Sharon felt as if her heart and head were going to explode, a rush of dizziness that terrified her, fearing she might swoon and thus be helpless when the madman came for her.

Within a span of two minutes or less her family had been annihilated, one shot each, and she had watched it from her place inside the barn, their slayer moving closer now to double-check his handiwork and finish off the job.

She couldn't stop to grieve now. It would be the death of her. And fighting off a marksman with the tools at hand—a broom and pitchfork—was so ludicrous it almost made her laugh aloud, hysterically.

The good news, if there was any: the killer had not seen

her yet, concealed as she was by the barn's interior shadows. If she could find someplace to hide…

But where?

The answer came to her before her would-be executioner had halved the distance from the point where she'd first glimpsed him. It was so ridiculous, and so revolting, that Rose felt the crazy laughter rising in her throat again. She choked it down, turned from the ruin of her life in the farmyard, and sprinted for the barn's backdoor.

If she was fast enough and pulled it off, the privy might just serve her purpose, but it wouldn't be enough to simply squat inside and pray the madman would forget to check it out. No, that was the crazy part of Rose's plan, her stomach roiling at the very thought of it.

The barn stood in between her and the gunman as she made the dash to reach her only sanctuary. Once inside the outhouse, with its door closed at her back but left unlatched—the obverse was a fatal giveaway—Rose held her breath and raised the privy's seat on its hinges.

A stench rose up to gag her from the pit latrine below, accompanied by lazy buzzing from a swarm of flies. Rose swallowed back the bile and ripped two pages from the old Sears Roebuck wish book mounted on the wall with twine around a nail, to serve for wiping.

Now, the pages had to double as a mask shielding her nose and mouth.

There was an awkward moment as she scrambled down into the reeking pit, then reached up overhead to ease the hinged seat down. Darkness descended on her misery and Rose began to pray, convinced that nobody was listening.

2

Wallace Mahan finished topping off the fuel tank of his Ford Model A, then replaced the gas pump's nozzle in its cradle on the left side of the Polly Gas dispenser featuring the likeness of a parrot sitting on its perch with one foot raised as if to grasp a cracker that the talking birds habitually squawked about in Walt Disney's cartoons.

The filling station stood on Wichita's southern outskirts, the downtown stretch of Sedgwick County's seat and largest city in the state of Kansas still a mile or more ahead of Mahan on his journey going nowhere.

Nowhere so you'd notice, he corrected silently, frowning. But I ain't done yet.

Not by long damned shot.

The Model A had gotten him this far despite its age and the mileage displayed on its dashboard odometer. Mahan had bought it new, back in December 1927, when Detroit unveiled it to replace the venerable Model T, America's best-selling motor car since its premier some twenty-seven years ago. Mahan had been a youngster in his early twenties then, new to a job he hadn't realized would change his life and ultimately blow up in his face.

He was still standing, though. Still moving forward like his Ford, a man his younger incarnation wouldn't recognize if they passed on the street today. Hell, looking in the mirror when he shaved, he sometimes didn't recognize himself.

So what? he thought, fishing inside one of his trouser pockets for the dollar eighty-one he owed from filling up the Model A's ten-gallon tank. With any luck, he'd put two hundred miles behind him before he was forced to stop for fuel again.

Now, all he had to work out in his mind was which direction he should head from Wichita.

It pissed him off, hunting a man whose name and whereabouts remained unknown.

The gas station's attendant and mechanic was a thirty-something man in faded Polly overalls, with hands so often stained by oil they'd never quite come clean. Scrub them until the skin was raw, apply steel wool around the fingernails, and someone who had never met the grease monkey could guess his occupation at first glance. His upper lip supported a toothbrush mustache, reminding Mahan of that Hitler fellow who was busy raising hell in Germany.

The station had a Zenith radio behind its counter, dubbed a "tombstone" by some people for its blocky wooden cabinet. Mahan had none inside his Ford, due to the added cost of having one installed, but he remembered listening to an old RCA at home in Lubbock, Texas, back when he still had a home and family.

All gone now, with his life committed to the road.

He paid up for his purchase, gave no thought to tipping extra, while a mellow-voiced newscaster finished talking about FDR's New Deal, some program coming up the White House called "social security," then segued into crime.

"Police still have no leads on last week's shocking murders of a family in Lyon County," he was saying, "with three people shot and mutilated on a farm outside of Olpe, Kansas. The survivor of that massacre, still unidentified while officers seek next of kin, is presently recovering from injuries sustained."

"Where's Olpe?" Mahan asked.

"How's that?"

"Olpe, in Lyon County. What the news reader was saying about people killed."

"That's up in Lyon County," the attendant said.

"I just said that. I'm asking *where*."

"Um, I don't get up that way much, but if I had to guess, I'd say ten miles or so south of Emporia, the county seat."

"And how far is Emporia from Wichita?"

Mahan had road maps in the Ford but wanted instant answers now.

"Well, if I had to guess—"

"A guess is fine."

"I'd guesstimate it's ninety miles or so, northwest."

Mahan turned on his heel and exited without another word, left the mechanic staring after him and wondering what kind of screwball he'd just waited on.

No matter.

Mahan cranked the Model A and rolled out of the Polly station before its attendant had a chance to read his Texas license plate.

Northbound, he passed a road sign telling him the city's population at the last census, five years ago, had topped one hundred and eleven thousand souls. Most of the ones still working, Mahan knew, would be connected one way or another to the city's dozen oil and gas refineries, spawned by gushers in the days before a War to End All Wars set Europe blazing and moved on from there across Asia and Africa, encompassing the world.

Mahan had registered for that apocalypse but was exempted due to being married at the time, and father to a child, besides which logged as an "essential worker" with the Texas Rangers. Over time, his wife had given up on him, he'd lost his daughter, and he was on leave from service with the Rangers, half expected by his captain to retire.

Mahan still had his badge though, even if he lacked any legitimate authority.

And he still had one final case to solve, unless it killed him first.

***

Mahan had passed through Kansas more than once, retrieving prisoners for extradition back to Texas, once on a vacation while his marriage lasted, but he'd never been to Lyon County and knew nothing of its history. The truth be told, he didn't care about it, either, only hoping someone there could point him toward the crazy bastard he was hunting down.

According to a highway sign he passed while leaving Wichita, the gas pump jockey had been nearly right about their distance from the city that some locals called "Doo-Dah" for no apparent reason. He'd guessed ninety miles, and it came out to eighty-nine, shaving a fraction off the travel time Mahan had estimated at his Model A's top speed of forty-five miles per hour.

That didn't save him much, but he would take whatever he could get.

He had been following the nameless lunatic for better than a year now, on his own, with no legal authority, though he'd been known to flash his Ranger's badge from time to time and leave whoever he was questioning with the impression that he had the Lone Star State behind him. That was easier to sell since last year, when ex-Captain Frank Hamer had started working off the books for Lee Simmons, director of the Texas prison system, to break up the Barrow Gang. People around the world had read about how Hamer and his posse killed Bonnie and Clyde outside Gibsland, Louisiana, back in April 1934, and Mahan found that dropping Hamer's name into a conversation helped to ease his way across state lines these days.

He didn't think of that as lying, necessarily, just coloring the truth a bit. His badge helped sell it, with his dated I.D. card and the revolver that he sometimes carried in a fast-draw holster on his hip. If he forgot to mention the small arsenal stashed underneath the Model A's backseat, what was the harm in that?

Those guns were meant for one man only, and he kept them clean, well-oiled against the day when he might need them to complete his work.

There wasn't much to see along the road to Lyon County. Mahan passed through El Dorado, population some ten thousand, thirty miles northwest of Wichita, then lots of nothing that was mostly brown or gray, the land once lush with wheat, corn, hay and sunflowers wind-blasted now, laid waste by vengeful nature after years of drought and over-farming with heavy machinery.

It was a funny thing, he thought, how man could try to rape the planet for a dollar, but he wound up getting screwed himself.

Funny, that is, except for those on the receiving end.

And somewhere, in the middle of that epic loss, as if the planet's payback weren't enough, there was a madman running loose, preying on those who hung on by their broken fingernails, praying for rain.

Mahan needed a name, or at the very least a pointer leading to his prey.

From there on in, he knew what must be done.

***

The U.S. Highways system, although incomplete, was far from new. Construction had begun in 1926, three years before the Wall Street crash changed everything worldwide, the government attempting to bring order out of preexisting state and county roads, highways, and color-coded "auto trails" with partial funding out of Washington, linking the forty-eight United States by modern roadways speeding commerce and vacationers from one point to another.

Mahan, as a onetime Texas Ranger, knew as much about that Herculean effort as the average American, and more than most. The germ of that idea premiered in 1916, with the passage of a Federal Road Aid Act paying 50 percent of the cost for upgrading major roads, providing 43 percent of those were interstate highways. Two years later, Wisconsin numbered its state highways. In 1921 a cautious Congress scaled back funding to 7 percent of a given state's highways, but that hadn't stalled establishment of the New England Interstate Routes in 1922. By 1926 there was an embryonic web of numbered U.S. Highways from coast to coast, mostly renamed versions of established state, county and local roads, although projections from the White House estimated that final completion would require another three decades or more.

Numbering of U.S. Highways so far had been designated by the American Association of State Highway Officials, founded in 1914, its membership comprised of state Secretaries of Transportation. Feds came on board in 1924, renaming the AASHO as the Joint Board on Interstate Highways. Final approval of the U.S. Highway System as it presently existed didn't make its way out of committee till November 1926, when work had finally begun in earnest.

So far, Texas had twenty-four U.S. highways, Oklahoma boasted thirty-four, and Kansas likewise shared in part of thirty-four. Mahan had traveled over most of those in Texas and his share of Oklahoma's as a Ranger, either on patrol of fetching prisoners. Kansas was newer to him, but he followed leads on this, presumably his last case, anywhere they took him.

And when that was done…well, maybe so was he.

Mahan just needed time enough to find the bastard he was looking for and then be done with it.

"Please Lord," he muttered to himself, tasting hypocrisy like bitter gall, "just give me time."

***

Emporia, Kansas

The Lyon County courthouse was a blocky granite building on Commercial Street, running north-south through town after Mahan got off state highway K-14. He circled once around the block sizing it up, counting the entrances and exits, working out how he should play it once he went inside.

So far, during his private hunt, flashing his star had been enough to get Mahan an interview with active duty lawmen who, if not particularly helpful in all cases, had been courteous enough to hear him out, accept some version of the shaded truth he offered them, and at the very least to wish him well. There'd been no leads he could pursue to any end, of course, or else he wouldn't be in Lyon County now.

There'd be no monster still at large and killing innocents.

Mahan parked at the curb in front, diagonally, locked his Model A and went inside. He wore the badge pinned to his shirt, keeping it visible but left most of his weapons in the car. The only other things he carried were a sap in his hip pocket and a pearl-handled switchblade knife he'd taken from a punk in Amarillo some years back.

He didn't plan on needing either item here, but there was only so much personal security a cautious man could leave behind.

The sheriff's office was to Mahan's left as he entered a spacious lobby with a staircase rising to a mezzanine and courtrooms on the second floor. The other offices downstairs were labeled for a county clerk and treasurer, the last one last one housing undefined RECORDS.

The deputy on greeting duty in the sheriff's office was a human fireplug mounted on a stool behind a wooden counter with a telephone and not much else at hand. When Mahan entered, he was reading *True Detective Mysteries,* lips moving as if he was sounding out the words. A glance at Mahan's badge got him to push the magazine aside.

"Help you, Ranger?"

"I hope so." Mahan introduced himself, using the rank he'd left behind and hoping no one tried to verify it. "Hoping for a couple minutes with your boss."

"That's Sheriff Whitmore, but he's kinda busy on a case right now…unless you called ahead for an appointment?"

"Didn't know I'd need to see him till a little while ago, passing through Wichita." Mahan lowered his voice a notch to keep it confidential, even though they were alone. "I've got a hunch we're looking for the same fella."

That got a silent gulp out of the deputy, his Adam's apple bobbing up and down.

"Hang on a sec," he said. "I'll go 'n ask."

More like a minute passed before the deputy came back, looking relieved or worried, Mahan couldn't say for sure.

"Sheriff will see you now."

***

The sheriff dwarfed his deputy, six-four at least, and likely tipped the scales around 250 pounds, most of that corn-fed muscle, although he was working on a double chin. His square face had a sunburned look, or maybe that was stress from trying to police a county near three-quarters of Rhode Island's size, with close to thirty thousand citizens and roughly half of those residing in the county seat.

Just keeping drifters on the move could be a lawman's full-time job these days, and now the sheriff's people had a psychopathic killer to contend with, where successive jurisdictions had already tried and failed.

The sheriff came around his cluttered desk, big hand extended for a grip that stopped just short of knuckle-grinding. "Roy Whitmore," he said. "And you are...?"

"Wallace Mahan."

"You're at least five hundred miles from home. What brings you into Lyon County, Ranger?"

"Wish I could tell you it was a social call."

"Something to do with what happened in Olpe then, I guess." Whitmore pronounced it "alp," unlike the gas station attendant back in Wichita, who'd made it rhyme with "old pee."

"I'm afraid so, Sheriff."

"Take a load off," Whitmore offered, nodding to a straight-backed wooden chair that faced his desk, while circling back to settle in his larger swivel seat. "So, what's your story?"

Mahan kept it simple and redacted. "What happened in Olpe," he replied, pronouncing it the sheriff's way. "We've had two incidents like that in Texas. Farming families wiped out and things done to the bodies afterward. There's been two more in Oklahoma, one outside of Lawton and the other near Sapulpa."

Whitmore caught on. "So, they're heading north."

"Looks like it."

"I've not seen the paperwork on those jobs."

"No surprise there," Mahan answered. "Weapons weren't always the same, for one thing. And you know how locals are sometimes."

"Meaning we don't like sharing with each other."

"Sheriff, in McLennan County, Texas, calls his case a murder-suicide. Four dead. Another, running Tarrant County, grants a stranger was behind killing three people there, but won't connect it to McLennan's case. Same thing in Oklahoma. The Comanche County sheriff has an Indian locked up, claiming he's made a full confession to the massacre of five victims."

"But…?"

"I've looked over the supposed statement and its full of holes."

"And what about Sapulpa?"

"Happened on the line between Tulsa and Creek Counties. They've been tussling over it and getting nowhere. Four more killed. One sheriff blames it on a gang of hobos, while the other wants to round up Mexicans."

"You mentioned variations in the modus operandi," Whitmore said, not showing off exactly, but advising Mahan that he knew his job.

"Shootings," Mahan replied, trying to keep his voice steady, "and knife work, mostly on the women."

"And still moving north."

"I think so, yeah."

"And someone's got you on the road."

Nodding, Mahan replied, "That sums it up."

"Like Hamer, eh?"

And there it was. Mahan said, "Well, it worked that time."

"I know Texas is big," Whitmore allowed, "but that don't give you any pull in Kansas."

"No, sir. And I'm not trying to step on anybody's toes. Just going where the trail leads. Heard about your case in Wichita, just passing through, and thought it couldn't hurt to stop and ask."

"I guess not," Whitmore said. "But you're too late."

"How's that, Sheriff?"

"Topeka took the case away from us. Part of them trying

to build up a state police force that'll handle major crimes and track down mobile bandit gangs."

"So, when you say they took the case…"

"They're handling it now, and I'm invited to butt out."

"From what I've heard there was a living witness this time."

"She's up in Topeka, too. State master-minds are trying to decide whether she had a hand in it or just got lucky, if you wanna call it that."

"So, if I hope to have a word with her…"

"You'd ask Topeka," Sheriff Whitmore said. "I wish you better luck than we've had."

3

Back on the road again.

Topeka, the state capital, was fifty-nine miles northeast of Emporia as the crow flies, but crows weren't bound to follow state highways. To reach his destination without blazing any new trails, Mahan had to travel east on Highway 50 for twenty-eight miles into Osage County, then catch Highway 75 northbound for another thirty-nine miles into Shawnee County. Call it sixty-seven miles. That only added ten more minutes to his trip, but Mahan chafed at every second of it passing on his wristwatch.

The scenery had barely changed at all and wasn't likely to, unless the heavens opened up and dumped a gully-washer on the landscape—which might only make things worse at that point, washing off what topsoil still remained. And looking at that Kansas sky, advancing toward late afternoon, Mahan couldn't pick out a single cloud.

Topekans sometimes called their home "Top City," maybe shortening the name slang-wise or possibly because it was both the state's capital and most populous settlement, topping sixty-four thousand in 1930. That aside, Mahan had read somewhere—maybe paging through *Life* magazine—that the name translated from a phrase used by early Kansa-Osage tribal settlers meaning "a good place to dig potatoes."

Still, he guessed that it could have been worse. Chicago, with a census claiming fifty-three times the number of souls in Topeka, derived its name from a Miami-Illinois word meaning "stinky onion."

And from what he knew about the Windy City, there must be a germ of truth in that.

When Mahan crossed the southern city limit of Topeka, he pulled up outside an IGA grocery story and checked his map, confirming that he'd find the office he was seeking right downtown, on Southwest Seventh Street, east of Gage Park.

Kansas had nothing in the way of state police per se. In 1933, fed up with roving gangs of bank robbers and kidnappers, Governor Alf Landon had teamed with Highway Department Director Wint Smith to form a stopgap agency, consisting of ten Motor Vehicle Inspectors supervised by the State Highway Commission. Spread them out over eighty-two thousand square miles, chasing phantoms who raced across state lines at will, and what hope did they have of picking off one random killer who'd been at the game for well over a year?

Not much.

Still, if "the state" had taken over from the sheriff's men in Lyon County and the only living witness from the murder spree so far was in their custody, Mahan was bound to speak with someone in authority and find out what they knew, if anything.

He parked the Model A half a block west of his intended destination, locked it up, and walked down to the Motor Vehicle Inspection headquarters. It sounded like an agency designed to check the safety features on Blue Bird school buses, and he saw nothing on entering to disabuse him of that first impression.

Once again there was a counter separating a small lobby from the working area behind it, but with no one manning the reception desk this time. Mahan went up and tapped a silver call bell half a dozen times, until a paunchy officer came ambling over, belly straining at a Sam Browne belt with shoulder strap, over a short-sleeved shirt of baby blue and navy trousers. There was no gun on his belt, nor any indication that he'd ever handled one.

"Need something, Mister?"

"Texas Ranger Wallace Mahan. What I need's a conversation with the man in charge."

"And what's this all about?"

"A string of massacres that's made its way across three states and into Kansas now. The Lyon County sheriff tells me someone in this office has the latest case."

The deskman colored, maybe thought of something smart to say, then swallowed it and settled for, "I'll be back in a minute. Wait right here."

***

The deskman lied. He didn't come back in a minute—or at all, for that matter. Instead, four minutes passed by Mahan's watch before an older officer appeared, this one wearing a Colt New Service .45-caliber wheel gun with a six-inch barrel on his hip and an expression on his long face that suggested he knew how to use it.

The name plate on his short-sleeved shirt read BOLTON. Silver bars attached to collar tabs on both sides pegged him as a captain among Motor Vehicle Inspectors, for whatever that was worth.

"Who are you?" he demanded, barely glancing down at Mahan's star.

"I told the other officer already. Wallace Mahan, with the Texas Rangers."

"Anybody tell you you're in Kansas, Mahan?"

"I keep hearing that. And I keep hoping I'll run into someone of a mind to solve a string of murders that's left nineteen bodies in three states so far and shows no sign of letting up."

"What's any of that got to do with me?" Bolton inquired.

Mahan counted to ten. Said, "Do you want to talk about it in the lobby, Captain?"

Bolton thought about that for a moment, then said, "All right, come on back."

Mahan pushed through a waist-high swinging gate with no latch visible, piss-poor security, and followed Bolton's swagger to a glassed-in office at the bullpen's southeast corner. By the time they reached it, the desk officer had waddled back to claim his stool. A radio hissed static from the far side of the room.

Inside the semiprivate office, Bolton ordered, "Sit," like he was talking to a dog, and moved around a desk with files heaped in the middle of its blotter. Peering across them, he eyed Mahan for another moment, then said, "Okay. Talk."

Mahan leaned forward in his armless chair, with elbows braced atop his thighs.

"Three states, five counties, nineteen dead, with killing methods close enough to say they match." For emphasis, he said, "Nineteen *so far*."

"Suppose that's true," said Bolton, "and I'm not admitting that it *is*, mind you. You've got how many crimes in Texas?"

"Two attacks with seven dead."

"The other state you mentioned?"

"Oklahoma. Nine more killed in two attacks."

"And you say one bad boy has done 'em all?"

"He may not be alone, Captain."

"A gang, then?"

Mahan had to shrug at that. "There's been no living witness until Lyon County."

"Yeah…about that…"

"What?"

"I'm not convinced this girl who walked away wasn't involved somehow."

"Besides surviving?"

"Can't say yet. I've got her under observation, waiting for professionals to fill us in."

"Professionals, you say?"

"Head doctors."

"You think she's the *killer?*"

"Wouldn't be the first time that a teenager went nuts and killed their folks."

"A *girl?*"

The captain shrugged. "Maybe a boyfriend talked her into it. We're looking at that angle, too."

"You've got it wrong, Captain."

"Says you. These other killings, which aren't my concern, you said there's never been another victim who survived. How 'bout she's not a victim in the first place, but the doer. One of 'em, at least."

"I need to speak with her."

"The hell you say. What are you even doing up here, Tex?"

"My job, Captain."

"Uh-uh. Unless somebody changed the law and didn't mention it, your job ends at the Texas line."

"Not necessarily."

"You wanna spell that out?"

"I take it you're familiar with Frank Hamer." Playing that card, sure, if he had to.

"I've heard of him," Bolton agreed. "Sounds mostly like a headline-grabbing glory hound to me."

Mahan took one deep breath to calm himself. Replied, "My mama always warned me about talking shit on subjects where I'm ignorant."

Bolton's cheeks took on a tinge of angry color. "Mamas say a lotta things, some of 'em true and others not so much. I'd bet she never told you one day you'd be chasing ghosts around in other states."

"I'm on assignment," Mahan told him, lying. "Going where the case leads."

"If your case leads you to Kansas, then you've got no jurisdiction. This is *our* case. Nothing says it's linked to anything went on in Texas, nor in Oklahoma, neither."

"That's why—"

"No. I'm done with this. Go home and take your fairy-story with you. If you don't…"

"What, Captain?"

"I might have to have a word with your superiors. Or maybe have one of our doctors look at you."

Mahan saw he was getting nowhere. Rising from his chair, he

told Bolton, "Well, thanks for listening. It's always nice, knocking ideas around with another professional."

He left the office door standing wide-open as he started for the street.

***

On his way back to the Model A, a voice called out behind Mahan.

"Hold up a second, will you, Texas?"

Mahan turned, hands curling into fists. He was fed up with Kansas condescension from a bunch of yokels who were blind to happenings around them.

Standing on the sidewalk, hand-rolled cigarette protruding from one corner of his mouth, the eye above it squinting through the smoke, another officer in baby blue and navy stood ten feet away. This one was armed like Captain Bolton, with a big Colt .45. The surname COOPERMAN crowded the nameplate pinned above his left breast pocket.

Mahan looked him over. Frowned. "Is there a problem, Officer?"

"I wouldn't be surprised, but not with you." He glanced back toward the agency's front door, then asked, "You have a car around here?"

Mahan nodded. "Follow me."

When they were seated on the Model A's front bench seat, Mahan at the wheel and watchful, in case Cooperman tried reaching for his Colt, the Ranger asked, "All right. What's up?"

"I heard a bit of what was said in Captain Bolton's office," Cooperman replied. "That glass ain't half as soundproof as he likes to think."

"And?" Mahan prodded him.

"The captain's not a *bad* cop once you get to know him, but the truth is...well, he's really not much of a cop at all."

"Meaning?"

"When the state created our division, it was meant to chase bad men. So, why'd they go and call us Motor Vehicle Inspectors? Can you tell me that? It isn't like we go 'round giving people speeding tickets. Spread thin as we are, we couldn't catch one of a hundred thousand traffic violators, even if we wanted to. Ten guys, for Christ's sake. I mean, what was on their minds?"

"Bolton's out of his league, you're saying."

"What they needed was a man in charge who knows his motor vehicles, considering the name they stuck us with. And Bolton's got that covered seven ways from Sunday. Till a couple years ago, the only thing he did was writing tickets. Moving violations, jaywalking, or if a license tag was out of date. His big investigations were collisions, mostly caused by someone driving drunk."

Mahan replied, "And what about yourself?"

"Eight years a street cop here in Topeka, here, before they transferred me and handed me a one-time hundred-dollar bonus. I've worked robberies and murders, rapes, you name it. Shot a fella one time, four years back, after he pulled a knife on me."

"How'd that turn out?" Mahan inquired.

"He died."

"It happens."

"Anyway, about this girl they're holding at the hospital..."

"She's injured?"

"Not the way you mean, and not that kinda hospital. This

one's Topeka State Hospital, meaning the asylum."

"Because Bolton thinks she killed her family?"

"That won't hold up," Cooperman said. "He's got no evidence, and she's been standing by her story from the first minute a trucker picked her up."

"Which is…?"

"She hurt nobody. Saw her parents and her brother shot, then hid out best she could and wound up being overlooked."

"But Bolton doesn't buy it."

"He's an easy answers kinda guy. That's how you get promoted, in Topeka, anyhow. Don't know how things are done where you come from."

"What's this girl's name?" Mahan asked him.

"Rose of Sharon Halliday. I seem to recollect she's seventeen."

"And Bolton's stashed her where, again?"

"At the Topeka State Hospital, on West Sixth Street."

"I should get over there," said Mahan.

"Can't today," said Cooperman. "You've missed visiting hours, and the kid most likely can't have any coming through, regardless."

"Shit!"

Cooperman frowned. Added, "Unless maybe the drop-in was a lawyer or a relative."

***

Stymied for the time being, Mahan saw he'd have to spend the night and get an early start next morning. That would also give him time to hatch a plan before he pressed ahead.

As Cooperman was stepping from the Model A, Mahan shook hands and thanked him for the information he'd provided. The patrolman shrugged it off, saying, "Feels like the right thing. If it winds up going south on you, maybe forget we had this talk."

"What talk?" Mahan replied and left him standing on the curb.

The first order of business: where to stay the night?

He'd passed some tourist courts on his way into town, clusters of cabins built around a parking area for motor vehicles, catering to mobile Americans who could afford to pay their way instead of hopping freights in trainyards or trying to cross the continent by thumbing rides with long-haul truckers. The clustered lodgings had been spreading out from coast to coast for ten years now, starting before the Wall Street crash, and out in California had been dubbed "motels"—motor hotels— although the nickname wasn't catching on yet once you passed the Rockies headed east.

One place Mahan had noticed, pulling into town, had been the Jayhawk Tourist Court on Southeast Lakewood Boulevard. It had a dozen cabins and a sign that boasted "CLEAN ROOMS" for a nightly rate of fifty cents, indoor bathrooms included. The Jayhawk also had a railroad dining car set off to one side, up on blocks, that advertised "GOOD EATS" painted above its row of windows facing on the highway.

Driving back to check it out, Mahan tabled consideration of tomorrow's plan for later, once he'd fed and had a shower or a bath, whatever was available for half a buck. It would be tricky, getting in to see this Rose of Sharon Halliday inside a state asylum, maybe under guard, but he would think of something once he'd cleared his head.

The Jayhawk's manager was pushing fifty, didn't seem to care for shaving, but was making up for it by going bald. He wore a string tie and a vest made from Old Glory, peering at the world through wire-rimmed spectacles whose bifocal lenses that made rheumy eyes seem half again their normal size. He greeted Mahan with a yellow smile and took his fifty cents while filling in a registration card and passing it across the counter for a signature.

Mahan signed "Adam Jones," retrieved a key to cabin number four, and went to see his room. The Jayhawk's sign was accurate enough, concerning cleanliness, although the furnishings were spartan and the bed's quilt threadbare. Taking in the bathroom, he found both the toilet and a claustrophobic shower spotless.

Fair enough.

Once he had checked the room, Mahan retrieved his suitcase from the Model A and left most of his guns concealed beneath the rear bench seat, well out of sight. The only piece he brought into the tourist cabin was his Smith & Wesson Model 27 Registered Magnum, a blue steel revolver with walnut grips and a 3.5-inch barrel that was short for target shooting but just right for pistol fights that Mahan had so far survived.

He kept the Smith & Wesson loaded .357 Magnum rounds, although it would accommodate less powerful .38 Specials just as well, their projectile diameter being identical. The difference was in the powder load: 321 grains of black powder propelled a .38 slug at nine hundred feet per second, while the Magnum round's extended casing, loaded with faster-burning rifle powder, dispatched its projectiles at 1,454 feet per second—capable of piercing auto bodies, sometimes cracking engine blocks, and penetrating metal vests that were no longer bulletproof.

Mahan concealed the Smith & Wesson underneath his pillow, left his suitcase on the bed, and double-checked the bathroom's window before locking up its only door and heading for the diner, anxious to explore the local definition of GOOD EATS.

A sign inside the place advised a newcomer to SEAT YOUR-SELF, dispensing with a hostess. Mahan chose a booth for two, its window facing on the Jayhawk's parking lot, allowing him to watch his Ford. A solitary waitress, past her prime and weary looking under hennaed curls, brought him a menu and delivered coffee, strong and black.

The menu wasn't anything he hadn't seen before while traveling, with minor variations from the cook's imagination. They had burgers, with or without cheese; chili with beans; soup of the day (beef stew that afternoon); fried chicken; pork chops; "lake-caught" trout (as if they could be netted from the sea); and a short list of steaks. Mahan decided he would split the difference, choosing a chicken fried steak, baked potato, and boiled collard greens on the side.

His meal arrived in something close to record time and lived up to the diner's ad outside. Mahan enjoyed it, took his time, and left a dime tip for the waitress as he walked back to his cabin through the early shades of dusk.

By then, he had conceived the rudiment of an idea for his approach to the hospital staff, but knew he'd have to play the better part of it by ear, depending on the asylum's routine for handling visitors. His badge might help, but Mahan thought he'd save it for a kicker, since it had no legal weight behind it outside Texas, even if he'd still been on the job.

Miriam Ferguson's election to a second term as Lone Star governor had been a kind of death knell for the Rangers. People called her "Ma" from the initials of her first and middle name—Amanda—and the fact that husband James was widely known as "Pa." He had been governor before her, from January 1915 until summer 1917, when was slapped with twenty-one impeachment charges, convicted of ten and removed from office. Miriam managed to rebound from that, elected as the state's first woman governor in 1924. She'd lost a reelection bid in 1926 to the attorney general who'd indicted her husband, then came back again to win a second term in 1932. By then, the Great Depression had reduced the Texas Rangers to a short-handed forty-five men, barred from travel statewide unless riding their personal horses or taking advantage of free railroad passes. Another dozen officers resigned, rather than serve under a Ferguson regime, with the remaining thirty-two assigned to a new Department of Public Safety, merged with the Highway Patrol.

Mahan might still have stuck it out, but private tragedy had changed his life and personal priorities, compelling him to hit the road and see what he could do to put things right. That proved a futile exercise, he understood today—some things, once broken, never could be mended—but he still clung to a private mission like that peg-legged Captain Ahab chasing a white whale.

Revenge.

After a tepid shower, Mahan got in bed wearing elastic-waisted undershorts and nothing else. His right hand found the Smith & Wesson underneath his pillow, comfortable with an easy grip despite the double-action pistol's lack of an external safety, trusting to experience and the revolver's trigger guard to keep his brains inside his skull.

Tomorrow, he decided, had to take care of itself.

Tonight, his overriding hope was that he wouldn't dream.

4

Mahan's Baby Ben alarm clock jangled him awake at half-past six. He dressed quickly in clothes that could have used a pressing, even after spending all night on a hanger to reduce their wrinkling from his suitcase and returned the Magnum to his Model A before he went to breakfast at the diner.

Henna-hair had been supplanted a younger brunette waitress who had hemmed her uniform an inch or so above her dimpled knees to give male diners on the early shift a little pick-me-up. Mahan returned her smile, accepted coffee, kept his order simple with a Denver omelet including diced ham, onions and bell peppers mixed it with the eggs. A side of hash browns filled him up and got him focused on the task that lay ahead.

His first job was to meet with Rose of Sharon Halliday if that were even possible and hear the story of her grievous loss first-hand. Mahan could guess some of the details from the other case files he'd perused, backed up by personal investigation of the Tarrant County crime, but details varied from one slaughter to the next, as if the murderer was scatter-brained in some respect or still feeling his way toward ultimate fulfillment of a ghoulish fantasy.

Aside from gleaning details of the latest crime, Mahan suspected that the slayer followed news reports of his activities, at least sporadically. Announcement that he'd dropped the ball and left a lone survivor at the Lyon County scene would come as a surprise, might jar him, though whatever happened after that, as a result, was still unknown.

Would the maniacal degenerate lose confidence, or maybe try to win it back, save face by jumping straight into another raid and proving he could do it right next time? Whichever way that went, the best Mahan could do was try to close the gap between them, narrowing the killer's lead, maybe devising some way to anticipate his next move.

And of one thing, Mahan was convinced.

The man he sought would never stop unless someone or something forced him to.

From reading up on other murderers who'd left a trail of victims in their wake and never were identified, Mahan supposed there could be several reasons why a lunatic stopped acting on his urges. Being jailed or sent to an asylum on some unrelated charge was one potential stumbling block. Disabling injury or death would be another. Certain maniacs, he guessed, might finally burn out and kill themselves, while nature or coincidence could deal with others, touching them with terminal disease or crippling them somehow, forced to give up the hunt.

The only ending that would satisfy Mahan was death by his own hand.

He'd come too far to back out now. Mahan would find the monster who had set him on his present course and finish it, if that turned out to be the last thing that he ever did.

Which might not be so bad.

He had a debt to pay, and after that, who gave a damn what happened next?

Finding Topeka State Hospital wasn't hard. He knew it was on West Sixth Street, thanks to his chat with Trooper Cooperman, and Mahan got its address from the telephone directory in his nightstand. The cabin had no phone, mind you, but he supposed the books were free and helped tourists maneuver around town. The drive took twenty minutes, workday traffic slowing Mahan down, and when he finally arrived, the layout took him by surprise.

The lunatic asylum could have been a castle overseas. Its redbrick centerpiece had rounded towers at its two front corners, varied heights, four stories on the left, five on the right, with conical roofs and windows aplenty, enough for a first-class hotel. Concrete steps rose to an elevated porch surmounted by a second-story balcony. Behind the central building and attached to it, five-story wings stretched off to either side, with spires rising from steeply sloping roofs, fronted by more windows galore facing the street across a manicured lawn. No stranger to the place would ever guess that people were locked up inside, some of them doubtless in straitjackets or some other kind of forcible restraints.

Mahan motored along the driveway from West Sixth, parked in a roundabout reserved for visitors, locked up the car and passed inside.

**

Before the tall door closed behind him, Mahan's nostrils caught the too-familiar smell of hospitals the world over—disinfectant mixed up in a losing fight with sickness and decay--that wiped out any first impression that the place might be a royal palace or a grand hotel inviting tourists to a pricey getaway.

Beneath those smells, he also picked up something else, a tang of desperation that might well have been imaginary, or some residue of bitter wasted lives.

This wasn't Mahan's first excursion into an asylum. Back in Texas, he had twice delivered shackled felons, judged not guilty but insane, for storage at the Wichita Falls State Hospital. He had a fair idea of what went on inside such places, ranging from group psychotherapy to "water cures" and electric shocks, on to lobotomies that disconnected portions of a patient's brain, purportedly correcting misbehavior while erasing various compulsions and eradicating memories. He hated the facilities that many people joked about—the "booby-hatch" or the "laughing academy"—when all he'd ever seen or heard from one of them were tears and screams.

A woman's voice distracted Mahan from bleak recollections, asking, "May I help you, sir?"

A nurse dressed all in white from short cap down to shoes and stockings stood beside a curved reception counter, watching him with wary eyes. Mahan supposed that visitors were few and far between, each unexpected drop-in a potential problem on the hoof.

"I hope so, Sister," he replied, approaching her and noting that she didn't offer him a hand to shake.

"We are a state facility," she told him primly. "I am not a nun."

"Apologies, and no offense intended, Ma'am."

"As to your business here…?"

He'd worked out this part in advance, a gamble, but he

41

meant to see it through. There was a chance that it would blow up in his face, but Mahan had considered all the angles and decided that the most he could be charged with up till now was simple trespass.

"I've received word that a niece of mine is here. She lost her parents recently, which makes me next of kin, her mother's side, although we haven't been in touch for quite a while."

A shadow seemed to pass across the nurse's face. Mahan supposed that the asylum couldn't have too many inmates who had recently been orphaned, but the rule book would provide for that eventuality. It also likely tipped this warder off to which patient he had in mind.

"The patient's name?" she asked him.

"Rose of Sharon Halliday. From what I understand, she's new here."

"And you are?"

Mahan had reckoned it was better not to lie about that, since a quick phone call to Captain Bolton would expose him anyway and make things worse.

"Wallace Mahan," he said. "She used to call me Uncle Wally. Mahan was her mama's maiden name."

The nurse digested that, then said, "Please have a seat. I need to find her doctor."

"I can wait."

She left him there, and Mahan passed on sitting down in one of the six wooden chairs that had been bolted to the lobby's floor, presumably to keep someone from going off half-cocked and using one to brain somebody else. Instead, he eyed a portrait of the hospital's director, mounted in an ornate frame, and wondered if he'd be confronted with the man in charge when the receiving nurse came back. A worse scenario might have the woman or her boss placing a call downtown and stalling Mahan while they waited for a team of Motor Vehicle Inspectors to show up and save the day.

If it went sour on him, Mahan planned to bluff it out as best he could, display his Ranger's star and bluster, even plead if necessary, till they threw him out or handcuffed him for booking on some minor charge.

The one thing he refused to tolerate was giving up without a decent try.

Approaching footsteps made him turn to see the nurse approaching with a tall, white-coated doctor twenty-five to thirty years of age. A stethoscope protruded from the left-hand pocket of his coat, not worn around his neck where it could wind up being used as a makeshift garotte.

The doctor's face bore no resemblance to the hospital director's portrait—a relief of sorts—and his nametag read "DR. RALSTON."

"Mister Mahan?" he inquired, when they were close enough to speak without raised voices.

"In the flesh."

This time a hand was offered, strong and dry when Mahan clasped it.

"And you've come about your niece, I understand? Miss Halliday?"

"The very same."

Ralston addressed himself to the harridan beside him. "Thank you, Nurse Valentine. You must have other pressing work to do."

She plainly didn't want to go, but sniffed, said, "Doctor,"

and departed, rubber shoe soles squeaking on the hospital's light gray linoleum.

"Before we see your niece, may I ask how you're holding up, Sir?" Ralston asked.

Frowning, trying not to make too much of it, Mahan replied, "It was a shock."

"Of course. And possibly a miracle of sorts that Rose survived."

"Sounds like it, from the little that I've heard."

"I don't know many people who'd have kept their wits about them, in the circumstances, but the way she saved herself..."

"I'm still not clear on that," Mahan said, truthfully.

"Hiding below the privy's seat until the killer left, apparently, then climbing out when he was gone and cleaning up before she hitchhiked into town."

Jesus.

"I haven't heard that part before, Doctor. You figure the police are wrong, then? About Rose having a hand in what went on?"

"I'm not an expert in such things," Ralston allowed, "but I *am* an alienist specializing in the field of criminal psychology. From what I know about the circumstances of this crime, and after speaking with your niece, I'd have to say that theory is far-fetched, at best."

"That takes one burden off my mind," said Mahan, truthfully this time.

"So, are you ready?"

"For...?"

"A word with Rose?"

***

Along the way to Rose of Sharon's room, they made what passed for small talk in a lunatic asylum. Mahan knew something about the hospital already, opened in the 1870s and full since then. There had been whiffs of scandal off and on over the years, until state legislators passed a law in 1913 granting judges the authority to force sterilization of "habitual criminals, idiots, epileptics, imbeciles, and insane." Most surgeons didn't relish that, but some had played along and four years later, an amendment to the law had dropped requirement of a court order, allowing doctors who were so inclined to neuter caged-up "undesirables" as they saw fit. A backlash was developing against that practice, but the operations were continuing, procedures carried out at roughly one per month.

Ralston stopped short outside a door that had been numbered 409 and drew a sliding hatch aside, peering through a window that was reinforced with wire mesh pressed between two panes of glass. He stiffened for a heartbeat, muttered, "What in hell?" and quickly plied his key.

Mahan stepped in behind the doctor, sizing up the tableau at first sight. Two orderlies in rumpled uniforms of gray stood facing one another from opposing sides of the room's narrow bed. Between them, cringing up against the whitewashed wall, a young women with bleak fear in her eyes looked to the doorway for relief.

"What's this?" Ralston demanded of the orderlies, one of them blushing while the other tried a sneer for size.

The taller of them ran a hand through slicked-back greasy hair, tried to adjust the sneer as he replied, "We got our orders, Doc."

"Which are…?"

"She needs a bath," said Greasy Hair. "She was resisting."

"Yeah, resisting, Doc," his sandy-haired partner agreed.

"You'd best be on your way now," Ralston ordered, standing back to let the pair slouch past him and away.

"Bastards," the patient muttered, starting to relax a bit, then asked, "What's going on?"

"Your uncle's come to visit with you, Rose," Ralston replied. "I'll just step out and let you talk a while."

***

"Uncle?" Rose of Sharon said, as soon as Dr. Ralston shut the door. "What kind of trick is this?"

"No trick at all," Mahan replied. "I heard about what happened to your family. Same thing happened to mine last year, in Texas. So far, you're the first survivor."

"Am I? Here you stand," she challenged him.

"I wasn't present when the freak murdered my daughter, granddaughter and son-in-law," said Mahan. "If I have been, he'd be dead now and your folks would be alive."

She played connect the dots in nothing flat and answered back, "So, now you're tracking him."

"I am."

"Come all the way from Texas for it."

"And I'll chase him all the way to Hell, if need be."

"Are you suited for it?" she inquired.

Mahan took out his badge and showed it to her, watched her eyes go wide. They were a pretty shade of blue.

"A Texas Ranger?"

"Was," he said. "It's not the first time that I've hunted down a mad dog."

"And you killed them others?"

"Some," he granted. "Some went to the chair at Huntsville, others have life terms to serve."

"But now it's personal."

Rose hadn't phrased it as a question, but he answered anyhow. "Damn right."

She nodded. Said, "I with that I could help you, but you may have noticed that I'm stuck in here."

"Might be a way around that, if we work together on it."

"Oh?"

"I'd have to run a bluff," he said. "It wouldn't be the first time, but I'd be a liar if I said they'd all paid off."

"You mean pretending you're my uncle?" Rose suggested.

"That was just to get me past the door, but there's a chance—maybe an *outside* chance—that we could pull it off between the two of us."

She frowned at that. "Seems like the cop in charge is bent on hanging me for murdering my parents and my brother."

"Captain Bolton," Mahan said. "I met him, and I wasn't much impressed. Your doctor isn't, either."

"Do you think that matters?"

"Might do. Then again, I've got the star. I got wind of this killer for the first time down that way, which makes me pretty sure you're innocent in all of this."

"I absolutely am. But if you're not a Ranger now…"

"First thing, Bolton or someone here would have to call Austin and find out I'm telling tales. They might not push it that far, once you tell 'em we're related, and we get a little bit of law on our side for releasing you into my custody. Likely won't hurt if they were worried about being sued for false arrest and jailing a bereaved minor. The newspapers have fun with stuff like that."

"And if they still won't let me out?" she pressed.

"My best guess is that they'll require you to post bond pending arraignment."

"Which I can't afford," Rose said.

"I'll swing it somehow if it comes to that."

"And if they still won't budge?"

He shrugged. "I'll find a sympathetic lawyer, call your Dr. Ralston as a witnesses, raising so much hell they'd rather let it go than look like idiots."

"All right. It's worth a try, at least. What can I do to help?"

"First thing, tell me about the day you lost your family."

"Not 'lost'," Rose answered bitterly. "Their lives were stolen from me while I watched."

5

When Dr. Ralston came back into Rose of Sharon's room, using his key, Mahan explained their plan to spring her out of custody with his assistance, if he'd go for it. The doctor listened, mulled it over, taking longer than seemed necessary to agree if he was on their side.

It came as a surprise to Mahan, then, when Ralston finally replied, "Why not?" To Rose, he said, "I'd stake my reputation, what there is of it, that Captain Bolton's allegations won't hold up. Whether he'll let you go on my say-so is something else entirely, now."

Thinking of others first, despite all she had suffered in the past few days, Rose asked him, "What about your job here, then?"

"Truth be told, I've been a square peg in a round hole from the start around this snake pit. Call it my last straw. I still can't promise that my word will make a difference."

"It can't hurt," Mahan said. "What's the procedure, now?"

"We have to go through Dr. Taylor," Ralston said, confirming Mahan's apprehension. "Ten to one he'll side with Bolton, counting on referrals from the state and trying to avoid embarrassment."

"How do we get around that?" Rose of Sharon asked.

"Your uncle's plan to link the other murders with your family's should get things moving. If you need to, go ahead and threaten litigation. I can back that with my resignation and a plan to blow the whistle on those goddamned worthless orderlies. Fighting to keep you here while facing molestation charges might shift Taylor off the fence, especially if he has any clue about how many times they've violated hospital procedures and the law."

"Doctor, I can't thank you enough for this." Rose started reaching for his hand, then pulled hers back, embarrassed, eyes downcast.

"Okay, then," Mahan said. "We may as well get started on that paperwork."

"And brace yourself for Dr. Taylor's wrath," Ralston advised. "It's not a pretty sight."

"He hasn't sampled mine," Mahan replied.

They exited the room and made their way back toward reception, stopping on the way while Dr. Ralston ducked into a closet and returned with clothes to take the place of Rose's backless robe. She went into the closet, shut the door and changed, emerging in a shirt and denim jeans that nearly fit her, over black-and-white Keds easily a size too large, but laced up tight enough that she could walk in them.

The same nurse that had greeted Mahan on arrival manned the desk as they approached, her painted eyebrows arching as if she's just seen a ghost. Leaving her place behind the counter, she demanded, "What is going on here?"

Dr. Ralston took the lead, replying, "As her doctor, I'm discharging this patient into her uncle's care."

"Doctor, you know that her commitment is involuntary! I shall have to—"

"Take it up with Dr. Taylor," Ralston finished for her. "Go and fetch him, will you, while we start the necessary paperwork?"

It didn't take Nurse Valentine as long to make it back this time, as when she'd left Mahan cooling his heels. Beside her, stepping out ahead as they approached the lobby, strode the hospital's director, Dr. Taylor, looking older than his portrait on the wall, fuming with stress.

"Dr. Ralston," the boss demanded in a steel-edged voice, "explain yourself!"

"I'm signing out my patient to her uncle's care, Doctor," Ralston replied.

"The hell you say. This person was committed by police authority, and—"

"Based on faulty information," Ralston interrupted his employer. "I'm prepared to testify that she's incapable of murdering her family."

"And I'm prepared to have you stricken from the Kansas medical directory. Our first responsibility is to the state police."

"You mean the Motor Vehicle Inspectors?" Mahan challenged him. "You have a car wreck needs investigating, maybe Captain Bolton's up to handling that."

"And who are *you*, exactly?" Dr. Taylor rounded on him. "By what possible authority—"

"This man's my uncle," Rose of Sharon answered back, although the question hadn't been addressed to her. "He's not about to stand by while you hang me for something I didn't do."

"The courts make those determinations," Taylor said.

"And they'll decide it on the basis of accumulated evidence," Ralston cut in.

"What evidence?" Taylor demanded.

"Take my testimony for a start," the younger alienist said. "Aside from diagnosis of my patient, there's the matter of your negligence in screening orderlies who are unfit to serve at best and criminal at worst."

"Outrageous lies!" The color in the hospital director's face was moving on past red toward violet.

Mahan decided it was time to show his badge again. Holding it up in front of Taylor's florid face, he said, "And we'll be adding the results of my investigation into four more massacres with sixteen victims spread across two other states. Try linking up my niece to those and see how long you stay in charge around this place."

Taylor half-turned to face Nurse Valentine. "Get Captain Bolton on the phone right now!" he snapped.

"And kiss your job goodbye," Mahan advised her. "You'll be out with Taylor by this time tomorrow once we file our slate of charges."

Silence settled on the lobby for a moment then, the nurse regarding Taylor, who in turn seemed to be stricken dumb. At last, he spat, "Have it your own way, then. Expect no mercy when it blows up in your faces. Dr. Ralston—"

"Let me guess," said Ralston, and surprised Mahan by smiling. "Am I fired?"

"For starters," Taylor said. "I hope you won't miss practicing in Kansas after this."

Echoing Taylor's words from earlier, Ralston replied, "We'll let the courts decide that, shall we, *Doctor*?"

"You're making a serious mistake, Ralston."

"My first was working here, for you. Now if you don't mind, I have discharge forms to finalize."

***

Exiting the hospital some fifteen minutes later, Rose of Sharon at his side and Dr. Ralston on his heels, Mahan was half expecting cruisers to be waiting for him, sent by Captain Bolton, but he saw no trace of any. At the bottom of the concrete steps, he paused and turned to shake the doctor's hand.

"What happens next for you?" he asked Ralston.

The alienist shrugged. "He's fuming now, but it depends on how fast he cools down. In theory, he could raise hell with the Kansas Board of Medical Examiners or even take it to the AMA, but that means public hearings, testimony in the press, and scrutiny of how he runs this place. A wise man wouldn't push it, but you never know."

"I didn't count on dragging anybody else down with me," Mahan said.

"Don't worry. This was overdue as far as I'm concerned," Ralston replied. "I don't know what the two of you have planned—" he shot a sidelong glance toward Rose—"but you should get away from here as soon as possible, in case he gripes to Captain Bolton."

"I was thinking that, myself," Mahan agreed, not giving anything away as far as what he planned from there.

In fact, he barely had a plan at all, but didn't feel like saying that out loud.

They shook hands all around and finished saying their goodbyes, but not before the girl rose on tiptoes to plant a chaste kiss on her doctor's cheek. Ralston was blushing as they walked to Mahan's Model A and he opened the rider's door for her.

"Okay," she said, as Mahan gave the Ford's ignition key a turn. "Where next?"

"I'm thinking Lyon County if you're up to it."

She paled at that. Asked him, "There won't be any bodies, will there?"

"No," Mahan replied. Not sugar-coating it, he felt obliged to add, "I don't know where they are right now, but all you'll find at home are memories."

"Let's go, then. I can't get away from those."

Mahan had put the Model A in first gear, then hesitated, creeping forward twenty yards or so before he stopped again and set the parking brake.

"What's wrong?" Rose asked, then tracked his gaze and muttered, "Oh."

"Hang on a second," Mahan said. "There's something I forgot to do."

***

The orderlies from earlier, in Rose's room, were standing underneath a Shumard oak beside the driveway, smoking, hunched in what appeared to be an earnest conversation. Mahan stepped out of his Ford, checked his back pocket as he crossed a strip of lawn to join them in the shade.

The one with greasy hair glanced up and saw him coming, blinking once and growling to his friend, "Aw, shit!"

Mahan approached them with a smile fixed on his face, but there was heat behind it.

"Listen, Mister," Greasy Hair began to say, but Mahan

interrupted him.

"I just wanted to thank the pair of you," he said, "for taking good care of my niece."

"Say what?" the other asked.

"I'd like to shake your hands before I go," said Mahan. "Maybe write a commendation letter if you don't mind telling me your names."

It turned out that the two of them were even dumber than they looked. Grease Boy looked wary, but he still gave up his name, saying, "I'm Ricco Conti, with an 'i'."

"And Seamus Callaghan," his buddy said, relaxing into a lopsided grin that only held a smidgen of contempt.

Both stuck their hands out, waiting for the shake he'd promised them, and Mahan raised his own, but not for any show of friendship. It was weighted with a "convoy" black-jack, covered in black braided leather, with a lead weight mounted on a spring, eight inches long, a loop around his wrist to keep from dropping it.

The first swing clouted Ricco Conti on his left jawline and dropped him sprawling. Mahan spun before his first target was on the grass and followed through, unloading onto Seamus Callaghan's right cheek. When both of them were down and mewling curses, Mahan kicked each one of them in turn, punting their groins as if he hoped to score a field goal from the twenty-yard line. Callaghan threw up his breakfast on impact, while Conti simply squealed and hunched into a fetal curl.

Mahan stood over them and waited for their minds to clear a bit before he said, "When you can walk, go back inside and quit your jobs. Don't worry about giving notice and don't say a word about this while you're at it. If you try to hang around or raise a stink, I'll find you, and you won't get off so easy next time."

Leaving the pair of them to moan, Mahan walked back and slid inside his Model A. He kept his face deadpan until he felt Rose lightly touch his arm, then looked across at her.

"What if they try to charge you?" she inquired.

"Let 'em. I've got three witnesses to what they tried with you. Their butts will be the ones wind up in jail."

"So, should I call you Uncle Wally?"

"No," he said, and steered the Ford toward South Sixth Street.

***

Returning from Topeka to Emporia was simple. Mahan just reversed his route from yesterday, southbound on Highway 75 to Highway 50, then due west to reach the seat of Lyon County. Beyond that, he'd be trusting Rose to guide him south on Highway 99 to Olpe, population hovering somewhere around three hundred full-time residents, and over backroads to the farm where she had nearly died.

Easy, assuming they met with no obstructions on their way.

One problem might arise if Dr. Taylor beefed to Captain Bolton, leading to an all-points bulletin for Mahan and the girl. While possible, that didn't strike Mahan as likely, given the dispersal of state Motor Vehicle Inspectors across 105 counties, each man covering some eighty-two hundred square miles. All things considered that would be like looking for a grain of sand inside a sandbox.

Much more likely, if the hospital's director griped to Bolton, Bolton might phone down to Sheriff Whitmore in Emporia, but that struck Mahan as another dicey move. Bolton had pissed the sheriff off by laying claim to Rose's case, throwing his weight around, and as of yesterday, Whitmore was still resenting that. Bolton might have authority to make the county's top lawman back off from an investigation, but when it came down to Bolton ordering a search by Lyon County deputies, he would be whistling down the wind.

Mahan waited until they'd crossed the Shawnee County line into Osage before he asked Rose to relate her story from the top, including any details she could think of that might help identify the man who'd wiped her family off the map.

"That is," he added, "if it's not too hard to talk about."

"I want him worse than you do," she replied, then softened. Added, "Or I guess we both hate him the same."

"I'd say that's right," Mahan confirmed.

"And if I tell you my story, will you share yours with me?"

"Sounds like a deal."

She thought back to the last morning her family was still intact, proceeding from their simple breakfast to the routine chores that burdened any farmer's brood. Around mid-morning, Rose was getting ready with her brother for a cleanup in the barn, when someone pulled in off the highway, driving what she called a "fancy" car, but dirty from its travels in the Dust Bowl. Mahan asked about the make and model of the vehicle, but Rose was at a loss to fill him in. The only motor vehicle she'd ever ridden in had been her father's Model TT pickup truck, sold between 1917 to '27, ranking near the bottom of the "fancy" list.

"And what about the driver?" Mahan asked.

"I never saw him close up, but I wanna say he looked familiar to me somehow. Not his face or clothes, but something in the way he walked, carried himself. He stood up really straight compared to Papa."

"Any idea what he wanted?"

"Sorry, no. It looked like he was carrying a book, but what it was, I couldn't say. They didn't talk more than a couple minutes, tops, then he got back into his car and drove away."

"You never saw him come back after that?"

"I saw *someone*," she said, "but that was later, maybe fifteen, twenty minutes, and he didn't look the same."

"How close was he to you?"

"About a football field."

One hundred yards. At that range, if she didn't have binoculars or wasn't peering through a rifle's telescopic sight, the man's features would have been indistinguishable.

Mahan glanced at his rearview mirror. Still no cop cars rolling up behind them, and the highway up ahead was clear.

"What do you mean by saying that he didn't look the same, Rose?"

"Well…he seemed to be about the same height as the driver who pulled in, but this guy wore some kind of funny hat."

"How, funny?"

"Not like Papa's old slouch hat or the fedora Mr. Davies likes to wear around Olpe. As far as I could see, the brim of this one stuck out straight to either side and it was rounded on the top. I've seen its like before but can't think where or when just now."

"It may come back to you," said Mahan, hopefully. "What else do you recall about the way he looked?"

"He had a long coat on. I saw it flap below his knees and thought it was an odd thing on a day so warm."

"What was the first man who you saw that morning wearing?"

"An ordinary suit. Not Sunday best, I'd say, but with a tie and all."

"Color?"

"I'm thinking grayish, but he might've just been dusty, riding with the windows down."

"What else about the second man?"

"I couldn't see his face, but it seemed *wrong* somehow. Longer than normal, and it seemed blacked-out if that makes any sense."

"You think he was a Negro?"

"No, sir. It's more like he had a hood on, underneath his funny hat."

"Okay. We'll set that to one side for now. What else?"

"He had a rifle in his hands. It seemed longer than normal, too, but I can't tell you why."

"An estimate of length on that?" Mahan inquired. And quickly followed with, "Don't worry if you can't."

"I've thought about it," Rose replied. "I'm not so good at judging size from far off, but if he was six feet tall, let's say, the rifle must have measured five feet, easy."

Mahan tried to think of any shoulder weapon fitting that approximate description, quickly ruling out Winchesters and most other sporting arms. The only piece that he could think of was a goose gun, often made with three-foot barrels, meant for dropping birds from lofty altitudes. From there, he realized he'd never asked Sheriff Whitmore what kind of gun was used to murder Rose's family.

"All right," he said at last, and checked his rearview once again. "What happened next?"

6

Logan County, Kansas

The little caravan of homeless wanderers had stopped to spend the night on Highway 40 southwest of Winona. The next town farther on was Monument, an unincorporated flyspeck on the map that claimed to have a dozen residents against Winona's whopping three hundred and thirty-four.

A bunch of nothing in the middle of nowhere, much like the withered battlefields of France. Too reminiscent of another time when Death had marched across a barren landscape situated at Hell's doorstep.

It was getting on toward dusk. The soldier had already changed into his battle garb, with two exceptions from his last campaign. He'd swapped his Enfield rifle for another long gun and had added something new.

His choice of leading weapon for the raid he had in mind was a Browning Automatic Rifle, Model 1918, chambered for the same .30-06 Springfield rifle cartridges fired by his bolt-action weapon, but that was where the resemblance ended.

The BAR weighed nearly sixteen pounds unloaded, plus

another one pound seven ounces for a magazine of twenty rounds, against the Enfield's 9.2 pounds. Even so, it measured only twenty-seven inches long, compared to twenty-six for the bolt-action piece, its barrel shortened by two inches from the Enfield's twenty-six. Designed to bridge the gap between an infantryman's rifle and a light machine gun, it fired an average six hundred rounds per minute in full automatic mode, but also had the capability of firing single shots to keep from burning through a magazine within ten second flat.

Another difference between the Enfield and the BAR was their delivery of death on target. While the Enfield's makers claimed an optimum effective range around six hundred yards, John Moses Browning claimed his BAR was capable of killing out to fifteen hundred, depending on a shooter's skill and the adjustment of its rear leaf sight. Unlike the Enfields, BARs had no lugs for a bayonet mounting, although Winchester made a failed attempt by adding an experimental flash hider extension with bayonet lug to the weapon's muzzle.

The other changeup in the soldier's battle gear came with addition of four Mk 2 fragmentation grenades hooked to his pistol belt by means of curved safety levers that AEF warriors had nicknamed as "spoons." The Mk 2 had evolved, of course, from a Mk 1, dubbed a "pineapple" for thirty-two serrations on its iron casing that vaguely resembled the tropical fruit, designed for transformation into jagged shrapnel upon detonation in combat.

Designers of the Mk 1 called it the "simplest," yet most "fool-proof" hand grenade produced at its debut in 1917. To use one of the bombs, a soldier pulled its safety pin, pushed off a cap on top of the grenade, then pitched it, which released the "spoon" and started a timed friction fuse sizzling toward detonation within four to five seconds. Despite hyperbole from manufacturers, some problems were encountered on the battlefield, resulting in the Mk 1 hand grenade's withdrawal from service. A Mk 2 model then replaced it by war's end and was available through various black-market outlets to civilians such as gangsters who had used it widely in Chicago's bloody "Pineapple Primary" balloting of 1928.

The major difference between a Mk 2 and Mk 1 grenade: the former now had forty raised fragmentation knobs stamped in five rows of eight columns. Each bomb weighed one pound and five ounces, give or take a pinch of high explosive filling, and would kill or seriously wound unsheltered targets at a detonation radius of twelve to fifteen feet.

The hunter's chosen target was a deviation from his norm: three vehicles, all road-weary, that bore thirteen pilgrims—an unlucky number—on a journey westward to escape the Dust Bowl and, if prayers meant anything at all, to eke a better life out of America's broken society.

As luck would have it, though, their fate had been misplaced. Instead of supplicant wayfarers, they were fated to become part of a human sacrifice.

The lead vehicle in their little caravan was a Ford TT truck, designed to haul a short ton of cargo. It fit a driver and two riders in its narrow cab, with two more passengers in back, watching the miles pass by from threadbare padded chairs, surrounded by cheap suitcases and other items deemed too precious for disposal, with a tarp strung overhead at need to shield them from the elements.

Next up in line was a sand-blasted four-door Chevrolet National, with precious little of its once-green paint still visible. Debuted in 1928, it had survived for seven years as nature tried to wear it down and seated six, counting the driver, with assorted smaller items packed around the riders' feet.

The last vehicle was the newest of the three, Ford's Model B, a roadster premiered only three years earlier but used hard without much concern for keeping up appearances. A driver and one passenger took up the front bench seat, with more bundles plus sundry odds and ends shoved in behind.

The soldier had pursued his prey for two days, after spotting them outside WaKeeney, Trego County's seat. He'd noticed that they didn't seem to be in any all-fired rush to reach their journey's end on the Pacific Coast, pausing at highway rest stops where they'd do wash in the sinks and patronize the public toilets till some cop showed up and hustled them along. Around sundown or earlier, depending on their mood, they'd find some place to camp that wasn't posted off limits to trespassers and build a fire or two to warm them through another night.

This one would be their last.

The group consisted of four men, four women, and five children raged in age from three or four to roughly twelve years old. The adults made up two couples who'd spawned the kids, two single men and two young women who seemed unattached, although one slim brunette he'd noticed welcomed the attentions of a burly balding male.

All clearly sinners, they were marked for sacrifice and ripe for butchering.

***

"C'mon and have a sit-down, Addy," Raymond Pilcher said, patting the ground beside him underneath an eastern cottonwood.

Beyond the tree and silhouetted by the caravan's camp-fire, Adeline Grant looked nervous, even though their secret meetings had become routine over the past few weeks, since meeting on the long road west. She kept her voice down to a whisper as she answered, "I don't want to make a spectacle."

"Nobody's looking," Raymond told her. "No one cares."

He didn't quite believe that, but they were both single and both of age—in some states, anyhow, though Ray wasn't entirely sure about Kansas.

Not that he gave a damn right now.

At last, not quite reluctantly, Adeline joined him and sat down touching-close, where they could watch the three vehicles parked at roadside and detect at once if anybody was approaching. Full dark wouldn't overtake them for the best part of an hour yet, but Raymond had a way of spotting partial cover for their trysts.

Back at the cars, the other dozen travelers were finishing their meager evening meal and picking up the cans they'd opened before heating pork and beans, sweet corn, and Dinty Moore beef stew.

Hard times, but they were getting by so far. And at the moment Raymond didn't care about his stomach's pangs.

He leaned in for a kiss and at the same time placed his right hand over Adeline's left breast. She seemed about stop him, then her hand cupped over his and pressed him closer to her through the gingham fabric of her blouse. Raymond could feel her nipple, tweaking it and loving how she trembled at his touch.

A little more of that, before he reached under her calf-length skirt, hoisting the calico above her knees and homing on the juncture of her thighs. She moaned into his mouth as

Raymond eased a finger under the elastic there and stoked her inner heat.

"Oh, Jesus, Ray!" she whimpered.

"He ain't here," Raymond reminded her.

"Someone might *see* us!"

"Makes it all the sweeter, don't it?" Probing, stroking, bringing in a second finger as she started shivering. "That's it, Baby. Just lie back now and—"

When the early evening exploded with a crash of thunder, Raymond jerked his hand back, sat bolt upright, gaping at the caravan. The Ford truck's bed was burning, bright flames twice their campfire's size consuming bedrolls, hammocks, whatever was heaped back there.

"Raymond?" Adeline's voice was quaking now, but not from lust. "What's going on?"

"Hush up!" he hissed at her. "We gotta hide!"

***

The soldier timed his pitch and dropped the Mk 2 frag grenade exactly where he wanted it for maximum effect. Its detonation shattered windows in the Model TT's boxy cab and set fire to whatever they were packing in the truck's bed, shrapnel fragments punching through the Chevy National's windshield where it was parked, a few yards back behind the Ford, screening the Model B roadster from taking any hits.

Before the echoes of that blast had died away, he had the BAR shouldered and spitting death among the campers, skilled enough from practice with the automatic rifle that he had no trouble milking three- and four-round bursts from it, instead of burning through the magazine in one ear-splitting rush.

He'd seen two of his targets making off together toward the shadows, as they had the last two nights, but didn't let that worry him. It left eleven targets in the open, pretty much, and he would take down all of them before he finished.

There'd be no loose ends this time. Not like the girl he'd somehow missed in Lyon County during his last raid.

That hitch still haunted him, an oversight he still didn't completely understand, which might propel him toward the gallows or whatever means Kansas employed to rid itself of murderers. Newspapers and the Studebaker's radio would only say she had "concealed herself" somehow, but how could that be possible, as thoroughly as he'd scoured the scene?

Focus, he thought, and brought his mind back to the present, taking care to make no more mistakes.

The first two pilgrims he cut down, a man and woman, were just rising from behind the campfire when his thirty-aught-six slugs punched through them, red spray trailing from them as they dropped like ragdolls on the highway's verge.

From there, he tracked left, caught a lean man dressed in overalls gaping at the Ford TT truck in flames, ripping two bullets trough his chest and slamming what was left of him against the driver's door.

It wasn't easy, counting shots on auto fire, but practicing had helped. The soldier guessed there were some fourteen rounds remaining in the rifle's magazine and caught a woman fleeing toward the Chevy, dragging one child with each hand. He barely had to aim while squeezing off his next burst, half a dozen rounds dropping the runners in a tangled snarl of twitching arms and legs.

Still breathing, possibly, but they weren't going anywhere.

That gave him six, with seven more to go counting the interrupted lovers. Call it eight rounds left inside the BAR's fat magazine before reloading was required.

Rising from where he'd taken cover, coming up behind the caravan on foot from half a mile due west, the soldier closed in slowly, cautiously. There was a chance that one or more of his intended sacrifices might have packed a firearm for their trip, and he was only mortal after all.

At least, so far.

Whether or not that changed, once he'd achieved his final goal, remained a mystery. There was at least an outside chance that he'd be disappointed, never mind how firmly he believed.

Another target, female, rose behind the Chevy National and took off running westward in a panic. Leading her a yard or so, the soldier stroked his rifle's trigger lightly, leaning into its recoil as two rounds howled down range. He couldn't swear that both arrived on target, but one must have, from the way the runner's flopped over toward her right shoulder, blood spurting from her ruptured neck.

Seven, with maybe six rounds left.

He stitched a line of holes along the Chevrolet and Model B, hoping to spook whichever of the caravan's survivors might be crouched behind them, praying that the storm would pass them by.

Good luck with that.

His plan paid off, four runners bursting out of cover, running for their lives. The man carried a child, three young ones crowding him and sobbing as they ran. It almost felt too easy, strafing them from thirty feet or so and blasting them to tatters as they fell.

And that left only two.

He pulled the BAR's spent magazine and stuffed it down inside a pocket of his overcoat, reloading with a fresh one as he closed in on the campfire, chambering the first of twenty rounds. No longer fearing any armed resistance, focused solely on completing what he'd started before any other motorists passed by, he called out through his gas mask toward the trees across the road.

"Come out, come out, wherever you are!"

The crazy part was that they *did* come out, and they were even holding hands, like teenagers surprised by Mom and Dad coming home early, caught necking instead of boning up on history or civics.

"Please don't," the young woman begged through tears.

"It isn't up to me," the soldier answered, sighting down the barrel of his BAR.

***

Returning to his car, the soldier stayed well off the pavement, ready to unleash a storm of fire on any vehicle that might approach. That wasn't part of his original design, but any warrior worth his salt prepared for all contingencies.

Pacing along beside the blacktop, clear of drifting smoke now, he imagined being back in France, at Belleau Wood during the Spring Offensive, or at the Meuse–Argonne two months later. He had made it to Vittorio Veneto before gas and shellfire took him out of action, but the memories were with him even now, despite passage of seventeen long years.

The war and his recuperation from it had opened the soldier's eyes to Destiny, disguised to him by piddling "normal" life before his baptism by fire.

Nothing had been the same since then, and never would again.

Once he had recognized the mission God intended for him, everything had changed. He had a purpose now, immutable, beyond the petty laws of man. No other living person had the wherewithal to understand him, be they pastor, priest, bishop or cardinal, even the Pope in Rome himself. Corruption, rife within all churches of the world today, prevented those not personally touched by God from understanding holy orders etched in fire and blood.

Only one man alone could change the world.

The first attempt, two thousand years before, had clearly failed to set things right with platitudes and parables.

Force was required, delivered one stroke at a time.

Back at the Studebaker, packing up his gear, the soldier could not have explained why he was chosen from among two billion souls on Earth, nor did he care. The torch was his to bear, and he would carry it until God, in His wisdom, either judged the work to be complete or struck him down and chose another champion to take his place.

7

Emporia, Kansas

Mahan and Rose talked pretty much nonstop during the ninety-minute drive back from Topeka to Emporia, except for when he stopped to fill the Model A's tank at a Texaco station in Lyndon, halfway down toward meeting Highway 50 westbound. Rose went off to use the washroom there and came back urging Mahan to avoid it if he could.

No problem there.

Before they reached Emporia, Mahan still watching out for Motor Vehicle Inspectors' cars, switching to scan for sheriff's cruisers once they'd crossed the Lyon County line, they'd covered the preceding crimes in Texas and in Oklahoma, focusing more than Mahan appreciated on his private loss, but knowing it was necessary for the bonding process or whatever somebody like Dr. Ralston would have labeled it.

His daughter, Nora Mahan Lester—named for a maternal grandma on her mother's side—was married to a Benbrook farmer, Thomas Lester, and had borne their only child, a son, two years before Mahan's wife Vera had her fill of Ranger's hours and whatever else was making her unhappy all the time, deserting him in such haste that demanding alimony must have slipped her mind. She had remarried six months later and was Vera Jacobs now, helping her new man run a grocery in Dallas. Mahan's grandson, Thomas Lester Jr., had been three days from his eighth birthday when some deranged son of a bitch dropped by and tore their world apart.

Mahan could quote the Tarrant County sheriff's summary of crime scene evidence from memory, the words emblazoned on his brain. Nora and her husband had been shot down with a .45 Colt automatic pistol, Tommy Senior in the barn, Nora apparently as she ran from the house to find out what the racket was. With that done, Mr. X had gone inside the house, found Tommy Junior hiding underneath his bed, and dragged him out to stab him thirty-seven times. A state pathologist suspected that the wounds were meant to form a cross between the boy's chest and his pubis, but with so much damage suffered by so small a corpse, he couldn't say for sure.

That done, the bastard had gone back outside and gutted Nora like a fish but hadn't bothered Tommy Senior any further. Shooting him twice in the face was seemingly enough.

"I'm sorry for your loss," Rose told him, when he'd finished laying out the facts.

"And I'm sorry for yours."

Two sorry people on the highway, looking for a murderer who'd cut them both adrift from any vestige of a normal life.

Vera, naturally, had blamed Mahan for the killings, vaguely claiming that his Ranger's job had come around to bite him in the ass somehow, and never mind her running off to look for greener pastures in the hurly-burly of Big D, forty miles due east from where her child and grandson died. It *must* be Mahan's fault, because he was the man who wore a badge and gun, expected to keep every one of some six million Texans safe around the clock.

The worst part was that Mahan often felt that way, himself.

Two months before the Benbrook killings, death had struck outside of Hewitt, in McClennan County, claiming Joshua Bodine, his wife Virginia, and their two kids, daughter Sadie and her younger brother Duane. That time, the maniac had used a .30-06 rifle on the parents, then savaged their children with what seemed to be a bayonet, most likely mounted on the rifle's muzzle. That made lawmen think of shell-shocked World War veterans, but all the ones on record were locked up in prisons, in asylums, or in county drunk tanks at the time the massacre occurred. From there, suspicion naturally turned to Mexicans, but none among them fit the bill.

The third crime was reported two or three days after it occurred, in January 1935. The Wardlaw family had tried in vain to make a go on thirty acres midway between Lawton and Fort Sill, Comanche County, Oklahoma, but their crops had blown away for two years running. Jackson Wardlaw was prepared to pull up stakes and join the other Okies fleeing westward, wife Jolene in tow, with their three sons—Jack Junior, Ephrem and Cheyenne—but hadn't made the move yet when the roof came down on top of them.

All five were shot that time, the .45 again, with knifework on Jolene and two of the three boys. In that rampage, the freak had gone after their eyes, as well as other mutilations with a blade about six inches long and double-edged. An alienist from the Norman State Hospital thought the crime "might have" some twisted motivation based on sex but couldn't specify a diagnosis. The Comanche County sheriff seemed to think it might be redskins on the warpath, but he got no further chasing that notion than McClennan County had with disappearing Mexicans.

Five weeks before the Halliday attack in Kansas, the killer paused again, south of Sapulpa in Creek County, Oklahoma, where a family of four had somehow caught his roving eye. Frank Norman was another hard-luck Dust Bowl farmer, weary of his battles with the weather but still hanging on with wife Constance and their two daughters, Amy and Francine. They'd never missed a Sunday sermon, trusted in the Lord to ultimately guide them through hard times, but He had let them down and sent a madman to their dying spread.

That time, as with the Bodine killings, he had used an aught-six rifle, though no effort had been made thus far to match it with McClennan County's massacre. Bullets had done for the adults, then Amy and Francine were cut to ribbons before death incarnate finally turned his attention to their mother's corpse. Creek County's coroner described the now familiar six-inch, double-sided blade, but nobody outside his jurisdiction bothered listening.

No one, that is, but Wallace Mahan, turning every waking thought and countless bloody dreams toward personal revenge.

***

When no one tried to stop them, driving through Emporia, Mahan explained his plan to Rose.

"It's getting late," he said. "I know a tourist court where we can likely stay the night. You'll get a cabin to yourself, or we can find some other place if they're sold out."

"I don't have any money," she advised him.

"Not a problem. This trip is on me. You pay your way by helping out as best you can, or if you think of somewhere else you'd rather be, I'll take you there and call it even."

"No," she said, watching the shops and offices pass by. "There's nowhere. Nobody."

"Okay, then. In the morning, if the sheriff hasn't turned up after breakfast, maybe you could stand to show me where your farm was—where it *is*, I mean—and walk me through what happened."

"Yes. Okay."

They reached the Jayhawk. Mahan turned into its parking lot and counted cars, doing the simple math to calculate there should be four cabins unoccupied. The same manager greeted Mahan like a long-lost friend, still hadn't shaved, still wore the same string tie and vest that seemed to be his daily working clothes.

"It's good of you to favor us again," he told Mahan. "Looks like you found a friend."

"My niece," Mahan replied, letting it drop there.

"Family's important, yessir."

"We need two cabins," Mahan informed him.

"Certainly." The guy abstained from winking, but it must have strained him. "You want those adjoining?"

"Doesn't matter," Mahan said, not liking what he saw behind the bifocals.

"All right, then."

Rose of Sharon interrupted, saying, "Closer's better."

"As you say, Miss. I've got numbers six and seven side by

side, or ten and twelve, with just a pair of honeymooners in between 'em. I can't promise they'll be getting any sleep," he added, and at last surrendered to the winking urge.

Rose turned away from him. Told Mahan, "Let's take six and seven, please."

"You heard the lady," Mahan said. He glowered hard enough to render any further repartee unwelcome, inked his name into the register and let Rose do the same, then paid up for the night. The manager passed keys to each of them in turn and wished them pleasant dreams.

Outside, Rose said, "He makes my skin crawl."

"Trust those first impressions."

"Sitting in there right now, thinking that we're…well… you know."

"Forget about him. He's beyond reporting anybody, and you won't have to lay eyes on him again."

They checked each room in turn to see which Rose preferred. Mahan waited outside while she examined both, found that the only difference was cut-rate artwork on the walls— both prints from Frederic Remington, one of a bronco buster and the other his famous "A Dash for the Timber," depicting red hostiles pursuing eight cowboys with one of them wounded.

"I'd like number seven," Rose said, "if you don't mind."

"Suits me. Any special reason?"

"It's farther from the office."

"I hear that. Want something to eat from the diner?"

"*He* won't be there, will he?"

"No sign of him when I had supper and breakfast there, last time."

"All right, then."

***

No patrons in the diner looked like newlyweds to Mahan. At the counter, two tall, stocky truckers hunched over their plates, an empty stool between them so they wouldn't jostle elbows. One booth held a gray man with a long face Mahan took to be a traveling salesman. In the next one, facing one another, a short man and taller, scrawny woman whispered back and forth over their meatloaf plates. It had the look of bickering.

Mahan and Rose sat opposite each other in the booth nearest the diner's entrance, Mahan sitting so that he could watch the parking lot and street beyond it. The same waitress from before delivered menus he'd already seem, filled Mahan's coffee cup, and told Rose that she'd be right back with a Coca-Cola. It came in the standard green glass bottle, with a cup of ice beside it, but without the cocaine that had been a standard feature of the "soft" drink before it was excised from the recipe back in 1903.

They ordered burgers—cheese on Rose's, none on Mahan's—with a side of French fries each and refills on their drinks. Between mouthfuls they made small talk and kept the volume low, involuntarily eavesdropping on the couple two booths farther back, who had begun to fuss at one another without trying any longer to conceal the fact.

"I don't recall my parents ever fighting," Rose said, when her second Coca-Cola had arrived. "I guess they must have, sometime, but I never caught them at it. Most folks do, I guess."

"Me and my wife—ex-wife, now—used to argue over everything, the last few years before she pulled up stakes. Always my fault, to hear her tell it. Maybe she was right. Who knows?"

"Before the end, after the bad times hit, my parents barely talked at all," Rose said. "I think that's worse than fighting, letting things build up and fester."

"I'm no expert," Mahan granted. "Otherwise…well, who knows where I'd be."

"Life makes no sense to me at all," Rose said, talking around the last bite of her sandwich. "First, you're doing fine, then something changes and you're on the skids. Turn around twice and everything's … just gone."

Back at cabin number seven, Mahan stayed out on the rubber WELCOME mat while Rose opened the door and stepped inside. She glanced back toward the office, seemed relieved to find nobody watching them, and asked, "So, what about tomorrow?"

"I was thinking of an early start," Mahan replied. "The diner starts to serve breakfast at six o'clock if that's all right."

"Like farming hours."

"Pretty much, I guess. Ten miles from here to Olpe, or a little farther. You can guide me on from there back to the farm. I mean…"

"Don't worry. I can take it," she assured him. "Justice is what matters now, whatever form it takes."

"Till six, then, and goodnight."

"I'll see you then."

***

Their cabins weren't adjoining in the normal sense, but with both bathroom windows open to the night, Mahan heard Rose running the shower as he brushed his teeth and shaved, getting a head start on tomorrow. He tried not to listen or imagine her under the shower's spray, but she made no sounds until she'd turned off the water.

That was when he heard her softly weeping, muffled sobs, not like the wailing he was used to at some funerals. Mahan experienced an impulse to get dressed again and go next door, try comforting the orphan any way he could, but nothing realistic came to mind.

And he imagined Rose wouldn't appreciate it if he tried.

Some things, Mahan supposed, were just beyond his capability—like managing a marriage on a Texas Ranger's salary and schedule, once the daughter who had formed his only lasting link to Vera had moved out to build a life away from hearth and home.

Where had that gotten her, except an early grave?

Sometimes Mahan believed her death, together with his grandson's and her husband's, *might* be partially his fault in some respect, although he couldn't pin it down to any certain thing. He would have bet his life the murderer was no one from his past, nobody who he'd sent to prison. Mahan calculated that he would have sensed the killer's sickness, even if the bastard hadn't started acting out his darkest fantasies and would have found a way to put him down like the mad dog he was.

Revenge made no sense to him, and in turn, that made the murders worse—random explosions like eruptions in a coal mine when a candle triggered lurking methane gas. That was the reason why he couldn't get inside the killer's head and think ahead of him, predicting where he'd turn up next and who his next targets might be.

Bitter frustration and futility.

A sharp twinge in his chest recurred, the first time in a

month of Sundays since he'd felt it twice within one day. Mahan went to the nightstand where his cheap alarm clock stood and took a vial of small pills from the upper drawer, palmed one and placed it underneath his tongue.

The medicine was nitroglycerin—known to the world at large as an unstable blasting compound that could detonate from careless handling, labeled glyceryl trinitrate by physicians who employed it to combat angina.

Chest pains to the layman, generated by a faulty heart.

Nitro wasn't a cure for angina or the deeper problems underlying it, but rather masked the overt symptoms and allowed a patient to pursue something resembling normal life. In Mahan's case, that root cause was congestive heart disease, occurring when the heart is unable to pump blood steadily enough to meet the body's needs. Aside from chest pains, it produced erratic blood pressure, shortness of breath, fatigue, swelling of feet and legs, climaxing in a fatal heart attack.

Mahan had heard a Houston doctor spell his likely fate out for him in the manner of a Gypsy fortuneteller reading tea leaves, but from X-rays and a range of other tests Mahan would never fully understand. The good news was, he didn't have to grasp the science. Bad news was the flipside, understanding that there was no long-term cure.

That didn't matter much to Mahan anymore, since Nora and his grandson had been snatched away from him by what some people labeled Fate, but Mahan called a monster cast in human form.

Mahan knew he might live another month, another year, or longer still. But all he'd focused on since Benbrook was the time required to find one final fugitive and take him down for good. Fair means or foul, it made no difference. Whatever happened to him after that, a medal from the governor of Texas or a lightning ride in Huntsville's death row chair, he didn't give a damn.

The job first, then to Hell with everything.

One shot could finish it.

And Mahan reckoned that Rose Halliday might be *his* best shot at success.

8

Mahan got through the night with no disturbance from the outside world, shocked into consciousness by his alarm. He had the best part of an hour until six o'clock and showered quickly before dressing, wishing the cabin had a radio that could inform him whether he was wanted by the law.

For what?

If someone meant to charge him, it would likely be for interfering with a state investigation. They could never make a case for him abducting Rose, and Mahan hadn't heard of anybody ever being locked up for impersonating someone else's next of kin, unless there was a forgery involved. As far as that went, Dr. Ralston had completed Rose's discharge papers and signed off on them. Before adding his signature and saying he'd watch over her—a promise Mahan meant to keep—he'd checked the document to satisfy himself there was no threat of perjury for posing as her nonexistent uncle.

On the doorstep to her cabin, straight up six o'clock, Mahan had raised his hand to knock beside the tarnished number seven, but Rose beat him to it, opening the door before he could. She wore the same clothes Dr. Ralston had provided from the hospital, of course—the only garments that she presently possessed—and Mahan made a mental note to take her shopping somewhere when they'd finished off their morning's work. Dark circles underneath her eyes betrayed a lack of sleep.

"I heard you coming," she said, stepping out to join him, turning back to lock the cabin's door behind her.

"Good ears."

"A relief," she said. "I've been jumping at little noises all night long."

"Today may help with that," he answered, but it sounded hollow even as he spoke the words.

Mahan stuck with the Denver omelet and hash browns. Rose ordered two scrambled eggs, ham and grilled mushrooms, with a short stack on the side. She caught him smiling as the waitress moved away and challenged him.

"What?"

"Nothing," Mahan said. Then added on, "It's good to see you getting back your appetite."

"Hunger isn't the same as feeling better," she advised.

He nodded understanding and surveyed the diner. Still no sign of any newlyweds, nor of the couple who'd been arguing last night. Another pair of truckers, different from yesterday, were seated at the counter, well apart. Down at the far end of the room, the maybe salesman had returned, same rumpled suit, working on breakfast with his back turned toward the entry door.

Their food arrived and they dug in. Despite all she had ordered, Rose beat Mahan to the finish line and washed it down with orange juice, telling him she'd never cared for coffee much.

"Something for everyone," he said. "If you need to do anything, before we hit the road…"

It was the closest he could come to mentioning the toilet, making it too personal.

"I'm fine." And then, on second thought, "A change of clothes would help, and I'll be needing some supplies in a few days, if we're still on the road."

Mahan was on the verge of asking what she meant, then he remembered Nora acting all embarrassed about Kotex in her early teenage years. Instead of questioning, he said, "Just tell me when and where."

Mahan dropped off their keys at the Jayhawk's reception desk, then drove a little over ten miles south on Highway 99 to Olpe, what there was of it. A sign that had been fading since they put it up in 1930, after the last census, claimed 317 inhabitants but only half a dozen showed themselves as Mahan passed through town.

Rose filled him in on local history. Olpe had been created as a railroad whistle stop in the late 1870s, at first called Eagle Creek Station, then renamed Bitlertown after a major local landowner. Some of his fellow Germans followed Bitler to the Kansas plains and later changed the town's name yet again, to Olpe, for the city most of them hailed from. Driving through town on Center Street, Mahan spotted a town hall, grocery and dry goods store, then Olpe was behind them, fading in his rearview as he faced more dusty plains.

"What now?" he asked.

"Jog to the right and get on Road L2," Rose said. "Another mile, mile and a half, you'll turn left on an access road, take that a couple hundred yards, and we'll be there."

"You're still okay with this?"

"I've seen the worst already," she reminded him. "There's nothing left."

***

He followed her directions until Rose announced, "We're here. Not much to look at, is it?"

"Most farms aren't these days," Mahan replied.

But she was right.

No gate identifying Aaron Halliday's abandoned farm, no fence in evidence around the property, no signs of life that Mahan could discern as he drove slowly toward the farmhouse and adjacent barn.

"Did you keep any animals?" he asked.

"Had a few chickens left," Rose said. "I'm hoping neighbors came to fetch them, so they didn't starve."

Mahan parked twenty feet out from the porch. While Rose got out to look around, he took the Smith & Wesson Magnum from beneath his seat and tucked it underneath his belt, around in back.

Rose noticed that and asked, "You think he might come back?"

"Unlikely, but you never know what might be hanging out on an abandoned spread."

"Abandoned. Right."

It was too late to modify the careless turn of phrase, so Mahan said, "You want to walk me through it?"

"Papa had me set to clean the barn with Tad. We were around behind the house and getting ready when we heard a car pull up."

"The fancy one."

"Uh-huh. Not new, nor clean, but it had cost a pretty penny not too long ago."

"Nobody in it but the driver?"

"Not that we—*I*—saw. Papa went out to meet him and they only talked a minute, but I couldn't hear what they were saying. Whoever the fella was, he had a book held out in front of him. Papa said something, shook his head, and then the other man drove off."

"What then?"

"I started on the barn with Tad. There wasn't much to clean except for sweeping dust, and that won't get you any-where these days, but we were working on it. Didn't want to seem like we were disappointing Papa."

"Then you saw the killer coming?"

"Yes."

They'd been all over that before, the stranger's long walk over open ground, and Aaron Halliday calling his wife to bring their shotgun to him from the house. He hadn't laid hands on it when the first shot came, and from the distance Mahan calculated, it wouldn't have saved him anyway. Shot-guns were made for relatively short-range fire, at men or varmints on the run, while an aught-six could drop a man at ranges better than three thousand yards—a quarter mile or more with open sights.

"The twelve wouldn't have helped him," Mahan told her.

"No."

After the first shot came a second, putting Rose's mother down, then brother Tad had run out screaming before Rose could stop him and a third round finished him. At that point, Rose had run out through the barn's backdoor, concealed herself in reeking filth below the privy, and thus saved herself from being victim number four.

Whether she'd ever purge the guilt of being a survivor was a question only time could answer.

"You did all you could," Mahan offered. "The only thing that made a lick of sense."

"I guess."

"I'd like to see inside the house now, if you don't mind."

"Follow me."

***

The farmhouse gave up no surprises. There were rusty-looking bloodstains soaked into the porch and wooden flooring of the entryway, but Rose had seen all that while it was fresh and barely faltered at it now. Mahan avoided stepping on the stains out of respect and didn't need to think about the wounds that had released that flood from Rose's mother and her younger sibling.

It was a carving on the door itself that stopped Rose short, gaping. A cross, still fairly fresh-looking, gouged with a knife's blade, and some scratches underneath.

"This wasn't here the last time I was," she said. "Someone's been back since then!"

"You're sure about that?" Mahan knew it was a foolish question, even as it left his lips.

"I've lived here from the time that I was born. Been in and out this door more times than I can count. This *wasn't here* before, and damn sure not the day my family was murdered."

"What's that down below the cross?" Mahan inquired. "Numbers of some kind?"

Rose bent down to peer at the small scratches, reading out, "G four fifteen."

"Does that mean anything to you?"

"It might," she said. "Considering the cross, I'd guess it's something biblical. Only two books in all the Bible start with 'G.' Genesis leads off the Old Testament. Galatians, one of Paul's epistles, comes up one-third of the way through the New Testament."

"Making the numbers chapter and verse," Mahan said, thinking back to his Sunday school childhood.

"Right. The fourth chapter could fit with either book, since Genesis has fifty and Galatians six."

"I don't suppose you've got a Bible handy?" Mahan said, half smiling.

"There should be one in what used to be my parents' bedroom, but I don't require it."

"No?"

"The Bible is the only book we ever read at home." Rose told him. "I've been through it front to back."

"And?"

"In Galatians, Paul is chewing out a bunch of wayward Christians for their sins. The fifteen verse of chapter four reads, "Where, then, is your blessing of me now? I can testify that, if you could have done so, you would have torn out your eyes and given them to me."

"You've memorized the Bible?" Mahan found himself amazed.

She shrugged it off. "In Genesis, the fifteenth verse of chapter four says, 'And the Lord said unto him, Therefore whosoever slayeth Cain, vengeance shall be taken on him sevenfold. And the Lord set a mark upon Cain, lest any finding him should kill him.'"

"Cain murdered his own brother out of jealousy, as I recall," Mahan replied.

"That's true."

"So, even though the Bible calls for murderers to die by execution, God was warning people to leave Cain alone?"

"That never made much sense to me," Rose said.

"But on the other hand, some of our killer's victims had their eyes cut out."

"I didn't think of that," Rose said. Her face had paled.

"Meaning he could be some kind of religious nut." He felt the need to quickly add on, "No offense meant."

"None taken. Religion's led to more folks being killed than any other cause that I can think of."

Mahan might have added race to that but didn't bother. He could see that Rose was pondering some other subject, possibly related to the first.

"You think of something else?" he asked her.

"Maybe so. It didn't come to me until just now. About three months before what happened here, another man stopped by. His car wasn't the same—smaller and cheaper—but its license tag said 'U.S. Government' above the registration number. Papa talked to him a while and said he was from something called the 'DRS.' I don't know what that is."

"I might," Mahan replied, and led her back into the open air.

***

"So, what's it mean?" she asked, once they had cleared the bloodstained porch.

"Unless I miss my guess," Mahan replied, "that's an abbreviation for the Drought Relief Service. Congress created it last year, in June I think it was, to help out cattle ranchers on the verge of losing herds to death from thirst across the Dust Bowl. Fellas from the DRS came out and offered low-ball prices for the steers in danger—fourteen, maybe twenty bucks a head—to set the ranchers up with spending money. If the rule of thumb from Texas carries any farther, roughly half the steers they bought were deemed unfit for rendering as beef. Those were destroyed and burnt or buried. The rest were cycled through another outfit called the Federal Surplus Relief Corporation, slaughtered with the meat passed around to poor families nationwide."

"Is that still going on?" Rose asked.

"Far as I know. The last I heard, while working with the Rangers, was that eight million and some odd steers had put over a hundred and eleven million dollars in the hands of farmers or their creditors and kept a lot of 'em from going bankrupt."

Rose seemed disappointed. "I guess that's a dead-end notion, then."

"Not necessarily," Mahan replied.

"Meaning?"

"It may connect somehow, if we can see it the right way."

"You think somebody from the government did this? Killed all those other people? Someone working for the government of the *United States*?"

"I didn't say that."

"Papa never had much use for anyone from Washington. He got into it once with Billy Lambertson, our congressman, at a town meeting in Emporia, claimed he was on the take from somebody or other and they almost came to blows, but

I still can't believe the U.S. government is sending killers out to slaughter folks on farms."

"They wouldn't mean to," Mahan countered. "And the man I'm after might not be a federal employee, but he could *know* one, get talking with his friend about which farming families were being hit the hardest or were easiest to reach."

"Jesus. Can you trust anyone?"

"A few," Mahan allowed, "but I keep whittling down the list as I get older. Pretty soon I'll have it down to me, myself and I."

"Don't cross me off yet, Uncle."

"Is your sense of humor coming back?"

"Maybe a smidge," Rose said, smiling, then she turned serious again. "Is there some way to check on what you're saying?"

"Possibly. I know an agent with the FBI, works in their Dallas field office."

"A G-man? Has he gunned down any bank robbers?"

"Not that I know of. If he had, Director Hoover would've claimed the credit for himself."

"I've seen him in the newsreels. He looks like a bulldog in a suit."

"And bites like one, from what I hear," Mahan replied.

"What would you ask this Dallas friend of yours?"

"I'm not sure yet. Maybe just tell him what I'm working on, ask him to sniff around a bit, leaving your name out of it."

"Suits me. Mr. Mahan?"

"What?"

"This man we're after."

"What about him?"

"Well, he killed your family, and even with that star you carry, you're not with the Rangers anymore."

"That's true."

"So, I'm just wondering, what will you do with him, assuming you can find him?"

Mahan feigned considering her question. Answered, "Take him back to Texas if he'll let me."

"I suspect he won't."

Mahan showed Rose his crooked smile. "I doubt I'll try too hard."

She nodded then. "That's what I hoped you'd say."

9

Kansas Highway 99

The Lyon County sheriff's cruiser started trailing Mahan's Model A approximately halfway back from Olpe to Emporia. The Ranger saw it rolling southward, past him, then his stomach lurched as the driver swung through U-turn in the middle of the road and rapidly accelerated in pursuit, the flashing red light on its rooftop coming on.

Rose glanced back at the squad car, muttering a curse that Mahan didn't have to hear.

"Let's just see what they want," he cautioned, pulling over on the highway's shoulder, switching off the Ford's engine. "It may be nothing."

"You can't let them take me back," she said.

As if they'd give me any choice, he thought, but kept that to himself.

The sheriff's car stopped close behind the Model A, just short of kissing bumpers. In his rearview, Mahan was surprised to Sheriff Whitmore himself emerge and take his time closing the gap on foot.

Mahan already had his window down for ventilation, looking up to say, "I didn't recognize you passing, Sheriff."

"Mahan." Whitmore stooped, looked past him, seeming disappointed when he spotted Rose. "Miss Halliday."

"Sheriff," she answered noncommittally.

To Mahan, then, the lawman said, "I got word that you might be traveling together, but I hoped it wasn't true."

"Captain Bolton," Mahan surmised.

"None other."

"Okay, Sheriff. What's the charge?"

Whitmore contrived to feign surprise. "No charge," he said. "The honcho back at the asylum had a change of heart on that. Nobody else has any evidence to pin our case on the surviving victim, much less any of the other killings out of state. As for yourself, Mahan, your alibi's as good as gold."

"So, what's this all about, then?" Mahan asked.

"I'm giving you a tip, is all. Another murder—well, a slaughter, really—that feels like it's up your alley. And the benefit for me is that it gets you both out of my hair."

"What's happened?" Mahan asked.

Whitmore responded with a query of his own. "You know where Logan County is?"

"I've got a map but couldn't answer that, right off the top."

"I'll help you out. It lies about three hundred miles due west of here. The county seat is Oakley. Sometime overnight, a crazy person or some vigilante—I don't know, and I officially don't care—shot hell out of a homeless caravan. Looks like he carried a machine gun this time, and my counterpart in Oakley thinks he might've tossed at least one hand grenade."

"How many?" Rose asked Whitmore, leaning forward.

"Thirteen dead, including kids," the sheriff answered. "No survivors this time. Stabs and slashes on the women and their children."

Mahan ducked his head and muttered, "Jesus," thinking of the carnage.

"Anyhow," said Whitmore, "if it *is* one fella doing all of this, looks like he's staying well ahead of you."

"That's it?" asked Mahan.

"Till he hits again. I'm hoping that's somewhere outside of Kansas and he never doubles back."

"I meant for us."

"Already said that both of you are free to go," Whitmore replied. "That means as fast and far from here as you can push this Ford. Turn up in Logan asking questions, and the sheriff's likely to reply in kind. His name's Caldwell. Don't say I didn't warn you."

Whitmore rapped his knuckles on the car's flat roof and walked back to his cruiser. Mahan watched him switch the red light off, pull out around the Model A and head back toward Emporia.

"Thirteen more dead. And children." Rose's voice was leaden. "What now?"

"I go on and see what I can learn. I can't advise you to stick with me."

"Where else would I go?"

"Be sure about this," Mahan said. "Protecting you may not be possible."

"I didn't ask you to. I'm staying after him."

"That means until the end, you know?"

She met his eyes. Answered, "I wouldn't have it any other way."

****

Logan County, Kansas

Mahan checked his roadmap after Whitmore left them, noting that the drive to Oakley was a trifle shorter than the sheriff had predicted, even with its two doglegs. Leaving Emporia, they traveled west on Highway 50 through Lindsborg, 50 changing into Highway 4 above that town of some two thousand souls, then north from there into Salina—ten times Lindsborg's population—and westward along Highway 40, passing nine more settlements of varied size before they reached Oakley.

Pit stops for gasoline and toilet breaks added more time to their itinerary in McPherson, Russell—where they also ate lunch at an A&W drive-up restaurant where carhops wearing roller skates brought them hamburgers, fries, and draft root beer—then once again in Quinter, as the sun was dipping low in front of them. Say seven and a half hours of traveling before they passed sign that read: OAKLEY, POPULATION 1,159.

That would be the 1930 census reading, and while Mahan guessed the city's head count had declined a bit over the past five years, it was a tossup. Oakley was the Logan County seat but also sprawled across adjacent borders into two more counties—Gove and Thomas—so he doubted that the last count was precise, by any means.

Their first stop was another tourist court, the Sunflower, where Mahan parked outside the manager's office and went inside, Rose on his heels. The registration clerk was twenty-odd years old and chunky, working on a sparse goatee that didn't seem to fit his oval face, cheeks scarred by acne that had plagued him until recently. He greeted them without enthusiasm, heard Mahan's request for two cabins, and shook he head.

"Can't help you there. One's all we got tonight."

"How many beds in that?" asked Mahan, feeling Rose's eyes upon him.

"One double," the clerk replied, "but I can get a folder in there for you. Costs another thirty cents per night."

"Let's do that, then," said Mahan. "What about a telephone," he added, glancing toward one mounted on the office wall.

"That's just for local calls," the clerk said, "with the charges added to your bill. You need long-distance, there's a booth outside, around the corner."

"Good enough for you?" Mahan asked Rose.

"It's fine," she answered, seeming not the least bit shy.

"Where can we eat?" he asked the clerk.

"Diner called Pete's would be the closest, four—no, five—blocks west."

"Okay, then," Mahan said. "Let's set it up."

They signed the register, received a key, and waited while the clerk retrieved a folding bed on wheels from a storeroom. "Linens and a couple extra blankets should be in your cabin's closet," he advised. As they were leaving, trundling it between them, he called out in a bored voice, "Enjoy your stay at the Sunflower. Come again."

Their cabin was the last of ten in line, extending eastward from the office. Mahan gave the key to rose, then shoved the rolling bed inside and told her, "Somebody I have to call, if I can still get hold of him. Just leave the bed till I get back."

Rose nodded. Said, "I'll lock the door. Just knock."

They hadn't driven into Mountain Time, which only covered four far-western Kansas Counties, leaving out three more immediately north and south of those. As always, Mahan marveled at the sort of bureaucratic mind that codified such nonsense into law but didn't let it trouble him. He checked his watch and noted it was 5:13 p.m.

Most office workers would be packing up and heading home by now, but not the FBI. Director Hoover had a rule that wasn't written down but still applied to agents under his command, expecting them to put in "voluntary" overtime each working day, regardless of their work on hand. A running tabulation let J. Edgar brag to Congress at appropriations time, noting the bundle he'd saved taxpayers by skimping on his agents' salaries. Mahan knew that was one reason why G-men were excluded from protection by the U.S. Civil Service. Likewise, Hoover could dismiss them on a whim, with some bullshit excuse, and those he fired had no recourse under the law.

With any luck, the agent Mahan hoped to reach would still be at his desk in Dallas, covered by the same Central Time Zone as Kansas. Standing in the Bell booth, wood and glass, he dropped a nickel in the pay phone's five-cent slot and waited for the operator, standing with a dogeared notebook in his hand. When she responded of the third ring, Mahan rattled off a Texas number and his party's name, identified himself using his now-invalid Texas Ranger rank, asking her to reverse the charges for his call.

The line hummed for the better part of half a minute, then Mahan heard ringing far away. A secretary—doubtless also clocking "voluntary" overtime—responded, fiddled with her switchboard, and a man's familiar voice came on, sighing to

97

himself as he agreed to take the call collect.

Six hundred some-odd miles away from Oakley, to the southwest, Agent Frank O'Neal said, "Wallace Mahan, as I live and breathe. Long time, no speak."

"Too long," Mahan agreed, then rolled the dice. "I need your help."

"Still riding that same hobbyhorse?"

"No getting off of it for me."

The FBI man sighed again, then said, "All right, damn it. What can I do for you, without getting my tit stuck in a ringer?"

***

Fifteen minutes later, Rose heard rapping on the door of cabin number ten. She She craxked the door an inch, its safety chain still on, recognized Mahan, and admitted him. He saw the made-up folding bed first thing, saying, "I told you I'd take care of that."

"It's nothing," she replied. "Besides, I'm taking it. You need more room than I do."

Mahan looked like he might argue, then he let it go and thanked her.

"Did you reach whoever you were calling?" she inquired.

"I did. An FBI agent in Dallas who I worked with off and on, while I was with the Rangers. Filled him in on what you said about the DRS man."

"Not accusing anybody," she reminded him.

"I made that clear, but still it's worth a look, if he can wade through all the red tape. Drought Relief's still operating, but employees shift around to other agencies," Mahan explained. "Between the Soil Erosion Service, the Civilian Conservation

Corps and Prairie States Forestry Project, Washington's been shuffling men around the Dust Bowl like the marbles in a game of Chinese checkers. Barring someone getting booted out for an unusual complaint, I wouldn't count on hitting paydirt."

"Sorry if I wasted everybody's time," Rose said.

"No, it was worth a try," Mahan assured her. "Still is, but I hate to get your hopes up."

"What about *your* hopes?" she asked. "You've been at this longer than me."

"I'm getting used to it."

"Oh, yeah?"

"Well, no. I guess nobody ever does."

"What did your agent say about the murders here?"

"I couldn't tell him much, but he'd already heard about them on the teletype. The FBI keeps track of things like that but won't step in without some federal crime being involved. Drive a hot car across state lines or rob a bank that's got insurance through the FDIC, they're all over it and post you as a public enemy. But kill twenty-odd people in a tri-state murder rampage and they've got no legal jurisdiction."

"That's crazy," Rose said.

"But it's the law. Besides, J. Edgar shies away from cases where he can't get headlines or the credit for convicting someone. Our guy, if and when he's caught alive, goes into state court and the trials could drag on for a couple years or more."

Her stomach growled, making Rose duck her head and blush.

"Sorry, with all this killing talk," she said, "but…"

"Say no more," Mahan replied, smiling. "Let's go find Pete's and see what kind of grub he's dishing up."

***

En route to dinner, they stopped at a pharmacy and sundries store on Highway 40, Mahan leaving Rose to pick out items that she needed, rounding a toothbrush and a tube of Colgate toothpaste, plain white underwear, an inexpensive nightgown and a box of Kotex. Mahan didn't like to think about some of the items on her shopping list, but gave her cash enough to cover it, then lingered by the exit until she had paid the tab.

"Sorry," she told him as they exited the store.

"No need for that," he said. "I had a daughter your age once upon a time, myself. A wife, too, if I can remember back that far."

Pete's diner was on par with the Jayhawk's, back in Emporia, but had a Wurlitzer jukebox at one end of the room, playing the Dorsey Brothers' "Lullaby of Broadway." That seemed out of place, but with the volume turned down low it didn't make much difference.

Their waitress looked to be of high school age or thereabouts, a blonde who had her hair cut in a bob and smiled a lot. Rose ordered up the meatloaf special, mashed potatoes on the side and succotash, with Coca-Cola. Mahan had the T-bone steak with what the cook called "Texas toast" but wasn't, and a roasted ear of corn, coffee to wash it down.

They made small talk while eating, nothing that related to the string of crimes, and Mahan felt a bit like an impostor—not just a civilian playing Texas Ranger, but a has-been lawman posing as an ordinary father on a road trip with his child. Two problems grated on him as he tried to keep up that charade: he was fresh out of live descendants, and Rose seemed to have no extant relatives at all—or if she did, it hadn't crossed her mind to mention them so far.

They finished off the meal with apple pie, then walked back to the Ford and started driving east again on Highway 40 toward the tourist court. Arriving at the Sunflower, Mahan removed his Smith & Wesson from beneath the driver's seat, Rose watching as he tucked it out of sight beneath his loose shirttail.

"Is that the only gun you brought along?" she asked.

"Not hardly."

"What else do you have?"

"A Winchester, a shotgun, and a couple other things laid by I thought might come in handy, one way or another."

"Hidden in the car, you mean?"

Mahan considered lying but it didn't set well with him for some reason. As it was, he cocked a thumb over his shoulder. "Backseat's hinged," he said. "I've got it latched down, but there's plenty room under the cushion."

"You don't want to bring them inside for the night?"

"I do all right with this," he said, patting the bulge under his shirt. "Too much explaining with the rest, if somebody gets wind of them."

"Okay. I guess nobody will be popping in on us."

Rose sounded like she needed reassurance. Mahan said, "Nobody knows we're here, right? Sheriff Whitmore's likely figured out we set a course for Oakley, but there's no percentage for him spilling it."

"Maybe your FBI friend?"

"Nope. I told him where the latest killing happened, but not where I am. He has to wait for me to call him back, since we've got no phone in the cabin."

"All right, then."

Mahan locked the Model A while Rose opened the door to number ten. He followed her inside and suddenly felt out of place, jumpy, remembering the first time that he'd shared a room with Vera in the days before they tied the knot, when they were still in love—or anyway, in heat.

Ridiculous, he thought, and felt warmth rising in his cheeks, turning away from Rose before she had a chance to see him blushing. She was barely half his murdered daughter's age, but he had watched her buying underwear, and now a twist of fate had put them in the same room overnight. He'd listened to her showering and crying only one night earlier.

Goddamn it!

"If you need to use the washroom, go ahead," he offered.

"I could stand a shower, but if you want to go first…"

"I normally do that and shave before I head out in the morning."

"Right, then. I won't be too long."

"Take all the time you like."

She shut herself inside the cabin's bathroom and he listened for the latch being engaged but only heard the soft click of the door closing. Mahan supposed that meant she trusted him, or at the very least didn't regard him as a threat.

Too old, a little devil on his shoulder told him. *And a good thing, too.*

He thought about which bed to take, but Rose had pretty much insisted on the folder and he didn't want to make an issue of it now. Mahan emptied out his pockets—wallet, pocket change, blackjack and switchblade—lining up the items on the nightstand where he'd placed his small alarm clock, set for half-past six a.m. He tucked the Magnum underneath his pillow, then hung up his shirt and trousers on a single wooden hanger in the narrow closet. That done, wearing his undershirt and shorts, he crawled under the covers on the double bed that would have been roomy enough on any other night, but now felt strangely cramped.

He kept his eyes closed, with his back turned to the washroom door when Rose emerged, not chancing any glimpses of her in the new nightgown, or maybe with a towel around her hair. Her movements rustled, whispered to him, almost felt like fingertips tracing his skin.

You damned old fool.

"It's all yours if you need it," Rose advised him. Meaning the bathroom, of course.

"Old men tend to get up odd hours through the night," he cautioned her.

"You're not so old," she said.

"You'd be surprised."

Tonight, he felt like eighteen going on a hundred.

"Sleep tight, then."

He smiled at that and answered back, "I'll do my best. Can't promise I won't snore."

10

Mahan woke before his travel clock could start to jangle, and he tried to keep the noise down as he shaved and showered, but he still found Rose already up and dressed when he stepped from the cabin's washroom.

"Thin walls. Sorry for disturbing you."

"It's fine. I never slept this late before…you know."

"I've always been an early bird, myself," Mahan allowed.

"So, what's our next step after breakfast?"

"I should check in with the sheriff. Someone must've called ahead by now, either that Bolton character or Sheriff Whitmore."

"What are you expecting him to say?"

"The usual. He doesn't want outsiders butting in on what's likely the biggest case he'll ever handle. He *especially* won't like you being in on it, so I should try and talk to him alone."

"You mentioned Captain Bolton. Is he likely to be coming here?"

"I'd say it's fifty-fifty," Mahan answered. "At the very least, he'll have one of his Motor Vehicle Inspectors horning in, most likely coming from Salina or Dodge City since they're spread so thin."

"I'll fight them if they try to take me back to that damned hospital," Rose said.

"Don't borrow trouble. I just want to see this Sheriff Caldwell. He won't tell me much of anything—won't mean to, anyhow—but sometimes what a person *doesn't* say tells you exactly what you need to know."

"Maybe he'll catch the killer."

"It's a nice thought, but I reckon he's already missed him, like the other cops he gave the slip to. That's including me."

"But you're still trying."

"Never cared for giving up."

After breakfast at a coffee shop a block from Pete's diner—no point in setting patterns that could work against them—Mahan took Rose back to the Sunflower, had her hang the PLEASE DO NOT DISTURB sign on their cabin's door. From there, Mahan drove to the Logan County courthouse on West Second Street. As often was the case with small and mid-sized county seats, the sheriff had his office and lockup adjacent to the courthouse, although not inside it.

Mahan, having left his Smith & Wesson at the tourist court with Rose, his sap and switchblade in the Ford, walked in unarmed and with his badge hidden inside a shirt pocket. The deputy assigned to morning duty on the desk was in his early thirties, muscular, his sandy hair crewcut in military style. His blue eyes studied Mahan up and down.

"What can I do for you?" he asked.

"I'm hoping for a couple minutes with your sheriff if he's got the time to spare."

"Your business being...?"

"The attack that killed a bunch of people recently, a few

miles west of town."

The deputy's right hand dipped toward his holstered side-arm without grasping it. "And who are you, sir?"

"Wallace Mahan, formerly a Texas Ranger, detailed to pursue the man responsible for similar mass murders down our way, then into Oklahoma and across the line to Kansas."

"You said *former* Ranger."

"Right. I'm off the clock on this job, like Frank Hamer on that deal last year."

"Bonnie and Clyde?"

"The very ones."

"Stand easy for a sec. I'll go see what if the sheriff's got time to discuss it with you."

Or the inclination, Mahan thought. But still, it was a start.

The deputy returned about five minutes later, motioning for Mahan to accompany him past the counter, through the bull-pen, toward an office in the rear that brought Roy Whitmore's bailiwick to mind. The door was standing open and the deputy said, "This is him, Sheriff," then strode away, his duty done.

A tall man filled the office doorway, bushy eyebrows doubly prominent below a hairline that was starting to recede. His brass nametag identified him as A. CALDWELL, while the rockers on his polished star read COUNTY SHERIFF. He stood around five ten and must have weighed at least one hundred ninety pounds.

Mahan considered reaching out a hand but settled for a verbal introduction. "Sheriff, I'm—"

"A onetime Texas Ranger," Caldwell interrupted. "Roy Whitmore already filled me in on you. He said you were… what was it, now? A pain in his keister."

"I'm working on my first impressions," Mahan said.

"And how's that going?"

"I'll get back to you."

Caldwell glanced down the hallway leading from his office to the bullpen. "What, no girl? I understand you have a minor traveling companion."

"Voluntary," Mahan said.

"Be careful crossing state lines with her. Somebody might get the wrong idea."

"They would be *seriously* wrong," Mahan averred.

"Well, now you're here, you may as well come in and take a load off."

Mahan followed Caldwell back inside the office, took a seat that looked and felt familiar, facing toward the sheriff's desk. Sitting across from someone in authority like that always reminded him of visits to the principal when he was back at school.

"It didn't take you long to make it over from Emporia, all things considered."

"But you'll find that I'm a stickler for speed limits," Mahan said.

"Just not for legal jurisdictions, eh? But what the hell. You're not a lawman anywhere these days. Fact is, you've got no more authority than any other John Doe off the street."

"Which still entitles me to make a citizen's arrest," Mahan replied.

"And how's *that* doing for you, so far?"

"I've still got a ways to go," Mahan admitted.

"Well, I'll make it easy for you. What you *won't* be doing in my county is examining what we call evidence. That means the bodies, vehicles, spent brass or anything else we've collected that ties into what's occurred. We're working on I.D.s for thirteen victims and we'll be releasing those names to the press *after* we've notified their next of kin, if we can track 'em down. You get nothing from my department. Wait and read about it the papers if you've got a nickel."

"Fair enough," Mahan replied. "You wouldn't care about a bit of news regarding Lyon County's crimes, I guess?"

"You ought to share that with Roy Whitmore."

Mahan forged ahead regardless. "I'm just wondering if there were any signs of possible religious motives at your crime scene."

Caldwell blinked at that, just once. "How'd you guess that?"

"It's not a guess, Sheriff. But if I'm wrong…."

"You're not. But if you breathe a word of this to anyone outside my office, I'll come down on you like forty tons of shit."

"Agreed."

"Two of the kids, both boys, were crucified after they died. The bastard tacked them up with roofing nails against the driver's side of an old truck, facing the highway."

"At the Lyons County scene," Mahan replied, "he carved a cross on the front door, together with a Bible reference. Likely from Genesis, fourth chapter, fifteenth verse."

"Likely?"

"Call it an educated guess."

"And that tells you…?"

"That he came back sometime after the murders, since it wasn't noticed on the day."

"Wasn't noticed by who?"

"The sole survivor. Sheriff's men."

"Uh-huh. And this is where you tell me I should have our scene staked out, in case he doubles back like to sniff around like somebody from Sherlock Holmes?"

"What would it hurt?"

"It wastes time I could use investigating. You remember what that is, from when you were a Ranger?"

"I'm just passing on a lead, like any citizen should do."

"Forget about it, Mahan. There's no scene left where he did his killing this time, just a stretch of highway. Cars are gone, bodies are gone, you name it. We know how to bag and tag potential evidence. My people didn't leave a cigarette butt on the site. I guarantee it. And our guy didn't leave anybody breathing by mistake, to come back later terrorizing 'em."

"All right then. Have it your way, Sheriff. You won't mind if I drive past the spot where you left nothing, I suppose?"

"Free country and a public highway," Caldwell answered. "If you're smart, you'll pass it while you're clearing out of Logan County."

"Thanks for seeing me," said Mahan. He left Caldwell glowering behind his desk and left.

***

Mahan drove back through Oakley from West Second Street to pick Rose up from the Sunflower Tourist Court. Before they left, he paid up for a second night, facing the goateed clerk alone so that the weasel didn't have another chance to ogle Rose.

"We're going to the place it happened?" she surmised, once they were underway.

"Unless you'd rather not."

"I've seen the worst that he can do already."

Mahan wasn't sure of that but let it pass. Instead, he told her, "Sheriff says there's nothing left to see. His people picked the highway clean."

"What are we doing, then?"

"I need to get a better feel for him, now that we know he's a religious man and sometimes makes another pass at crime scenes."

"Are you hoping we'll drive up and find him standing there?"

"I've never been that lucky," Mahan said.

"I think he came back to our farm because of me."

"How's that?"

"He must've known he missed somebody the first time around and it was eating at him. Maybe in his twisted mind he thought I'd move back in alone or come to fetch some of my things before I finally cleared out. I think he tried to put a curse on me or warn me that there's no place I can hide from him."

"If that's true, he was obviously wrong," Mahan replied.

"Was he? I'm trailing him right now, with you. We're heading for the very place he just killed thirteen people."

Mahan hadn't looked at it from that perspective. "Listen, if you've got someplace to go, just tell me, and I'll get you there."

"No, thanks. I'll stick with you. It's where I need to be."

"Well, if you're sure…"

"I change my mind, you'll be the first to know," she said. "Well, second, anyhow."

Caldwell was right. His people had left nothing at the slaughter site but scorch marks on the pavement where a vehicle had burned, some bloodstains on the verge and farther back, aswarm with flies and ants now. Mahan couldn't spot a single cartridge casing overlooked by searchers scouring the scene, nothing to indicate the killer had come back around to mark his turf.

"A waste of time, I guess," Mahan declared.

"Not if you got a better feel for him, like you were trying to," Rose said.

"I might have. Pulling off something like this tells me that he's unraveling a bit. Instead of moving on an isolated farm, he did it on an open road where anyone might come along. He kills thirteen, instead of just one family."

"You mean he's getting crazier," Rose boiled it down.

"Or else frustration from the last time pushed him toward a demonstration. A release."

"My fault, again," Rose said.

"Nobody's saying that, or even thinking it."

"I am," she argued back. "If he'd killed me along with Tad, Mama and Papa, those he killed here could be off somewhere in Colorado now and still alive."

"You start to think like that," Mahan advised, "and it'll eat you up inside."

"Too late. Are we about done here?"

"We are. I need to make another call."

***

Back in Oakley, Mahan stopped off at a Woolworth five-and-dime store located at Hudson Avenue and West Front Road. He handed Rose a dollar, shut himself inside a phone booth on the sidewalk, facing off toward railroad tracks, and placed another call to Frank O'Neal in Dallas.

Coming on the line, O'Neal said, "Pal, we can't keep meeting like this."

"Understood. I'll keep it short. Just checking in to see if you've learned anything."

"Not much," the G-man said. "Nothing to hang your hat on."

"Spill it anyhow."

"I wouldn't want to get your hopes up."

"Let me worry about that."

"Okay. I followed up your tip about the DRS and called a guy I know across the line here, in Fort Worth. He gave me a referral to their personnel department at the seat of government."

"The what?"

"That's what my boss calls Washington, D.C."

"Ah."

That sounded like something Hoover would say, making himself the chubby little spider at the center of a web that stretched from coast to coast.

"So, anyway, I followed up on that and got the number of a district supervisor by the name of Jacob Pollard." O'Neal spelled it out for Mahan. "He's in charge of handling 'difficulties,' as my contact put it, with their people in a tristate area."

"Including Texas?" Mahan guessed.

"Along with Oklahoma and Kansas."

"Where can I find this Pollard guy?"

"In Kansas City."

"Which one?"

"K.C., Kansas," O'Neal answered. "Not the one where our guys bit the dust at Union Station."

Yet another massacre, in June of 1933, but that one had been strictly Mob-related, even though the FBI's director told reporters there was no such thing. Shooters had tried to lift a fugitive from custody but wound up killing him, along with four lawmen. Two of the suspects had been slain last year, one by the Syndicate, one by the Bureau. Number three was on death row, awaiting execution in Missouri if his last appeals fell through.

"You have a number for me?" Mahan asked.

O'Neal gave him letters and digits, finished up by saying, "That's the federal building on State Avenue."

"I'm much obliged."

"You want to prove that, make believe we had this little chat."

"What chat?" Mahan replied, and cradled the receiver.

***

Rose met Mahan on the sidewalk. He asked, "Have you ever been to Kansas City?"

"Which one?"

"Either."

"No."

"I need to see somebody on the Kansas side, if I can set up an appointment. You're welcome to come along, or—"

"We've been over this," she said. "There's no place else for me to go."

"I couldn't take you to the meeting. That is, if I even get one."

"You can tell me all about it afterward. When do we leave?"

"Tomorrow morning, earliest. We're paid up for tonight at the Sunflower and I've got some other calls to make. First, the appointment in K.C., then touching base with other agencies around the area to see if they've got any open cases that smell like our guy."

"They'll talk to you?"

"Might do, if they get the impression that I'm still a Ranger."

"Isn't that a crime? Impersonating a policeman or whatever?"

"All depends on how you look at things. My badge number's legitimate. It's just retired."

"No skin off me," Rose said. "Whatever puts us closer to the trash we're looking for. But I'd prefer it if…" She stalled there, shook her head.

"Go on. If what?"

"Well, if you didn't get arrested, for example."

"Feels unlikely."

"Oh?" She arched one eyebrow, clearly skeptical.

"For one thing, most of 'em will never meet me in the flesh. They call to double-check with Austin, I'm long gone from Texas and they're not about to waste a Ranger's time running around behind me, states away from home."

"I'll take your word for that."

"Thank you."

"But try and be a little careful, will you?"

" 'Careful' is my middle name."

"Why don't I believe that?"

"Okay, then. It's Abner, but I wouldn't want that spread around."

She smiled at that. Said, "Who'd believe a psychiatric patient, anyway?"

11

Springfield, Colorado

The soldier missed his fancy Studebaker, but he'd bagged an-other car almost as good when he was leaving Kansas, from a hotel parking lot in Sharon Springs. His new ride was a Packard Twelve, new off the Detroit line in 1933 and labeled for its V12 engine that could generate two hundred horsepower, topping speeds of one hundred miles per hour. And it came with all the frills, from dashboard radio to a customized "air-conditioning unit" installed by a New York supplier.

Springfield is the seat of Baca County, the southeastern-most of Colorado's sixty-four political divisions. Settled in 1888 and incorporated the following year, Springfield was christened after the Missouri hometown of its founding brothers, boasting a present-day population a shade under fourteen hundred. Baca County, named for a 19th-century state legislator, was created in the same year Springfield was incorporated, but it hadn't drawn too many residents before the Santa Fe Railroad arrived in 1926, creating new towns and increased demand for agricultural products. As elsewhere in the Dust Bowl, that led to humanity raping the land, and when nature fought back, Baca had been among the hardest counties hit.

Even with that in mind, the soldier felt as if he might be straying from the focus of his mission. Kansas, now behind him, was a deviation from his personal crusade in two respects—allowing one stray victim to escape in Lyon County, thus potentially imperiling him, then reacting to that failure with a risky massacre outside Winona that compelled him to take stock of whether he had failed his Lord.

Not yet, perhaps, but if he didn't quickly bring his efforts back on track…

He was considering a plan to double back and maybe take his battle northward to Nebraska, then across the border into South Dakota and beyond. Perhaps he could duck into Canada along one of the old rumrunning trails and cool off for a while before returning to continue with the purge—but wouldn't that be spurning God, abandoning His holy sense of urgency in these End Times?

Perhaps while he was lingering in Baca County he should choose another farm at random and revive the method that had served him well until he went off-track in what was called the Wheat State before proud Jehovah chose another as an instrument of Heaven's wrath.

In Exodus 15 God called himself a "man of war." He emphasized that nineteen chapters later, saying that his "name is Jealous," although 1 John 4:8 said that "God is love," and some new-fangled versions of the Good Book claimed that "love is not jealous."

The soldier didn't let himself get bogged down in those

kinds of contradictions. He knew damned well that in the King James version, 1 Corinthians referred to "charity," not "love," and anyone who tried to put a mess of twisted words in God's mouth was a fool bound for hellfire.

Perhaps what he should do, instead of running off to Canada, was take a breather where he was, in Springfield. Find one of the harlots who were plentiful enough on downtown streets, around the city's several hotels, and introduce one to his Mark I trench knife, let her feel the righteous fury of a humble servant following directions from the Man of War on high.

The soldier felt a lazy stirring in his loins and took it as a sign from God Almighty, saying, "Go forth in My name and have no fear!"

What could he say to that, except, "Amen"?

***

Oakley, Kansas

Mahan called up Jacob Pollard at the K.C. federal building from a drugstore phone booth where he wouldn't have to raise his voice over the sound of traffic rolling past on Highway 40. Rose observed him from a distance while she looked over a chest-high rack of magazines with newspapers below.

A switchboard operator took his call and patched him through to reach a chirpy secretary or receptionist who answered, "Drought Relief Service. How may I place your call?"

Mahan decided that he might as well start lying right up front. "I'm calling for the Texas Rangers, trying to reach Jacob Pollard on a matter that we have under investigation."

Half true, at least, though the investigation wasn't going anywhere.

"And your name is?" the faceless staffer asked.

"Lieutenant Wallace Mahan, Company B, badge number 319."

"And the subject of your inquiry?"

"Murder spanning three states with no sign yet of stopping. I'll explain the rest to Mr. Pollard personally."

"Hold, please."

Mahan counted off the better part of two minutes and pictured Pollard reaching for a bottle in his desk before a male voice answered. "Agent Mahan, is it?"

"Ranger Mahan. Any agents that I ever met were federals."

"I stand corrected. You made some mention of homicides ongoing?"

"So far," Mahan answered, "there've been seven in Texas, nine more in Oklahoma, and sixteen this week alone in Kansas, close to where you are."

"Good Lord! Have any suspects been identified?"

"Not yet. That's why I'm calling you."

"What leads you to believe that I can be of any help."

"Connections to the FBI. An agent working Dallas tells me you're in charge of hires and fires for DRS employees spread over the states where we've had killings."

"Yes, that's true. But I don't see—"

"The killer messed up on his next-to-last attack so far. A victim who he meant to murder got away. That individual recalls one of your people visiting the farm in question roughly three months earlier."

"But still—"

"Our witness gave a vague description of the man. Remembers that he came on strong with preaching and got ordered off the place. Now we've been picking up religious symbolism at some of the crime scenes."

Pollard swallowed audibly, whether from nerves or gulping liquor Mahan couldn't say. The moment passed and he said, "I'd be happy to discuss this with you further, Ranger Mahan."

"I was hoping you'd say that."

"Unfortunately, I'm stuck in high-level meetings that begin in fifteen minutes, give or take, and will continue through the afternoon. If you could call me back tomorrow at, let's say—"

"I'd rather come to you. Learn more from looking subjects in the eye, I've found. Sometime the day after tomorrow would be good."

"You're coming up from Texas?"

"I'm in Kansas working on the latest murders, Mr. Pollard. I can make the drive from Oakley to your office starting in the morning and I'll see you the next day at…what time did you say?"

"Um…ten o'clock, perhaps?"

"I'll be there on the dot. And thanks."

Mahan rang off before the bureaucrat could change his mind, leaving no callback number for a cancelation when Pollard had thought about it more.

***

He found Rose paging through the latest *Newsweek* magazine and asked her, "Are you up to seeing Kansas City?"

"So, you got the meeting."

"Ten o'clock the day after tomorrow."

"Leaving when?"

"Right after breakfast in the morning. But if you'd prefer to wait here…"

"With the Billy goat? No, thanks."

"All right. You won't be in the meeting, but we'll find someplace for you to wait. Tonight's paid up, so we'll get started early. First, though, I still have a couple calls to make, then we can get some supper and turn in."

"Who's left to call?" she asked.

"Nebraska. South Dakota. Just in case our man's done other things we're not aware of yet."

"He needs to die."

"You'll get no argument from me."

Mahan called Lincoln first, Nebraska's capital and second largest city, holding off on Omaha, with close to three times Lincoln's population. As yet, there was no statewide law enforcement agency in the Cornhusker State, but Mahan calculated that Nebraska's two largest police departments would know something if a crazy man was wandering around and killing families.

Lincoln's chief of detectives took his call, and while he'd heard about "some recent trouble down in Kansas," there'd been nothing like it on the wires that his department monitored. The same was true of Omaha, although a young-sounding lieutenant took some notes about the other cases Mahan claimed that he was working on assignment out of Austin, jotting down the dates, the names that Mahan knew, together with the body counts. Because Nora was married and had taken Thomas Lester's name, that didn't sound a sour note.

The story was a little different from Pierre, the capital of South Dakota. Earlier that year, their governor, Tom Berry, made a move resembling Kansas with its Motor Vehicle Inspectors, recognizing that the home of Mount Rushmore—a marvel still in progress for at least the next few years—needed a unit to enforce its traffic laws and offer motorists emergency assistance in their travels, while advising them of future legislation on the drawing board. The best name Berry could come up with was the "Courtesy Patrol," mimicking Kansas when the force was limited to ten patrolmen. Each man drove a state-owned car, affectionately labeled "milk wagons," supplied with a tow chain, first aid kit, and a gallon can of gasoline. Each member of the team patrolled between two thousand and four thousand miles of blacktop roads and gravel highways. Their patrol cars had no radios, meaning each officer was forced to stop occasionally, calling in to headquarters from filling station pay phones.

Based on that, it came as no surprise that they had no records of similar attacks, but he'd expected none. A sergeant with a hacking smoker's cough got Mahan's name right on the second try but hadn't heard of any "weirdo" killings in the past couple of years.

He wound up saying, "And I hope it stays that way. This unit isn't up to handling anything like that. Do us a favor if you can and stop this prick before he heads our way."

"I'll do my best," Mahan replied.

"Can't ask no more 'n that," the sergeant said, and hung up in the middle of another coughing jag.

Rose saw him leave the booth at last and must have judged his mood by the expression on his face. "Nothing?"

"That's good news, I suppose," Mahan granted. "At least we seem to have a full list of his crimes."

"So far."

"They're on alert now, real cops in Nebraska and the

Courtesy Patrol in South Dakota."

"What's that?" Rose half smiled. "They check on people saying 'please' and 'thank you' to each other?"

"More like Captain Bolton's squad," Mahan replied. "Ten officers, like here, to cover the whole state and mostly help out drivers who forget to fill their tanks or get bogged down in mud."

"So, nobody."

"About the size of it. You hungry yet?"

"Whenever you are."

They tried a diner where they hadn't eaten yet, seeking variety. Mahan ordered a bowl of chili someone had filled up with beans, not even close to Texas style. It tasted all right, once he'd spiked it with Tabasco sauce, and there was ample cornbread on the side. Rose ordered a ground sirloin steak—essentially a hamburger without the bun—together with potato salad.

Back at the Sunflower they took turns with the shower, Rose first, neither of them saying much until they were prepared for leaving in the morning, after early breakfast.

They were both tucked in, lights out except for what leeched through their cabin's flimsy curtains, when Rose asked, "Do you think suspect Pollard fellow knows who's doing it?"

"I'll need to see his eyes in person, when I meet him," Mahan said. "He hesitated, maybe choked a little, when I mentioned the religious angle on the case."

"You mentioned there was none of that in Texas or in Oklahoma?"

"Not in Texas that I noticed, and I saw both crime scenes." Mahan blocked the memories of what he'd witnessed at the farmstead where his daughter, grandson, and his son-in-law were slain. "I couldn't get that close to both in Oklahoma—had to sneak up on one place at night, using a flashlight—but I could have missed it."

"Or it means he's getting worse," Rose offered. "Crazier."

"I'd hate to think what follows next," Mahan replied, though he already had.

"And Mr. Pollard has control of hiring people for the DRS, you said?"

"Hiring *and* firing. It's the second part I'm more concerned about."

"Because he might've noticed something, gotten rid of someone, if the other fellow started acting funny."

"Preaching to the farmers he was visiting or anything that might've led to multiple complaints. With Civil Service, you can't dump a worker over one or two mistakes. There has to be a line crossed, likely risking an embarrassment to Washington."

"But not a crime?"

"He likely would have been arrested then or held for observation anyway."

"Like me." Her voice was softer, almost muted.

"Not at all like you," Mahan replied. "Bolton went off the beam, accused you falsely."

"But I have a sense of how this person might be feeling if he was locked up."

"It likely didn't go that far. Governments like to whitewash problems if they can, without leaving a paper trail for some reporter to uncover. That freedom of the press thing in the First Amendment's more an obstacle than guidepost for most bureaucrats."

"Fire a crazy man and let him fester?"

"Wouldn't be the first time, if it happened. You can bet your bottom dollar it won't be the last."

"That disappoints me," Rose said. "Maybe I'm just childish."

"Or you wish that things were like somebody promised you in school."

"Guess I need to get over that."

"Or help to fix it where you can. That goes down one step at a time and never happens fast."

She thought about that for a while, then settled for "Goodnight."

Mahan echoed that sentiment and closed his eyes.

12

Kansas Highway 40, Eastbound

The drive from Oakley straight across the state to Kansas City spanned three hundred fifty miles, ten hours at the Model A's top speed when they could manage that, slowing for towns along the way, with stops for gas and lunch in Ellsworth, hear the halfway point.

The countryside was nothing Mahan hadn't seen before, but it still got under his skin, thinking of all the people who had seen their lives swept out from under them by towering "black blizzards" scourging the landscape, burying some people inside their homes and leaving more to die slowly from what the medics labeled dust pneumonia.

Topeka could have been a problem, situated sixty miles due west of Kansas City, but if Captain Bolton had his far-flung Motor Vehicle Inspectors watching out for Rose and Mahan, no one spotted them by chance or tried to stop them. Mahan started to relax a little when they'd passed beyond the capital, but wondered if some rude surprise might be awaiting them upon arrival in K.C.

Would Jacob Pollard have reached out to anyone after their conversation yesterday? He shared a building with the FBI and U.S. Marshals Service, both assigned to hunting fugitives who'd violated federal laws, escaped from prison, or skipped out on pending trials. In June of 1934 Congress had passed a group of laws imposing penalties on felons who crossed state lines while in flight from prosecution or confinement, but the crimes involved were federal: kidnapping, robbing certain banks, mail thefts, assaulting federal employees, shipping hot cars interstate.

Mere murders, even when the body count had mounted into double digits, only qualified if one or more of those who died had drawn a U.S. government paycheck. Otherwise, the killers—like the country's top-flight mobsters Hoover opted to ignore—were relegated to pursuit by state or local law enforcement agencies, within imaginary limits drawn on maps.

Mahan regarded that as an ass-backwards way of doing things, but at the same time, he knew many of his fellow Texans didn't want the FBI—much less the Treasury Department's revenuers—trampling on "states' rights." Sheriffs were chosen by election to police their counties, and if some of them were visibly corrupt...well, a dissatisfied electorate could either recall them or wait four years and try their luck with someone new.

From coast to coast, eighteen of the forty-eight states had established state police organizations, while ten more made do with highway patrols, some badly understaffed like those in South Dakota and Kansas, but theoretically empowered to investigate serious crimes. The other twenty states, just shy of half, were still considering the problem. Idaho had formed a state police force back in 1919, then dissolved it four years later when their governor decided that it wasn't working out.

K.C. had tourist courts around its fringes, but Mahan decided they could splurge for once on a hotel and picked one out that stood an easy fifteen-minute walk from the federal building where he was supposed to meet Pollard tomorrow morning. The nightly rates weren't terrible, but Rose suggested that they skip the bother of demanding two rooms and the clerk raised no objection once she'd signed the registry as Mahan's niece, adopting his last name.

Some cities these days made it criminal to register under false names, but Mahan had his driver's license and his Ranger's badge, while Rose professed that she was underage. The bottom line was cash, and Mahan had that covered, even though his stash was slowly dwindling.

At a pinch, he could have money sent by Western Union from his Texas bank, and if that source finally ran dry—well, maybe he would have closed the case by then.

If not, it wouldn't be from lack of trying.

Their room was a step up from the rustic tourist cabins they were used to, as it should have been at quadruple the nightly price. They had two double beds, no folding cot on wheels, and Mahan reckoned there was less chance of hot water running low. The also had a telephone, but he preferred the lobby's pay phone if he needed to call out of town about the case, avoiding any risk of hotel switchboard eavesdropping.

He *did* call from their room, confirming his appointment at the Drought Relief Service tomorrow morning, then they went to supper on State Avenue, surprised to find a restaurant that advertised "authentic Mexican cuisine." The decorations could have passed in Texas, and the smells emerging from its kitchen seemed all right, but Mahan kept his expectations at a minimum.

In fact, the quality of fare surprised him yet again. They took their time over tamales, enchiladas, rice and beans, then walked back to their lodgings as gray dusk settled over K.C.

***

They were up an at it early, having breakfast in the hotel's coffee shop, and Mahan reached the federal building fifteen minutes in advance of his appointment. A gray-haired receptionist in trifocals confirmed that Mr. Pollard was expecting him, offered him coffee that Mahan declined, and then directed him to several outdated magazines displayed atop a low table.

He chose *Time,* the most recent periodical at two weeks old, and flipped its pages without reading anything until a man's voice interrupted the charade.

"Ranger Mahan?"

Pollard was short, around five four, which made his bald spot visible to any taller persons who encountered him. He had a pince-nez dangling from a gold chain fastened to his vest and Mahan saw a pale circle around his left hand's ring finger, suggesting that a marriage had been terminated recently.

There was a lot of that going around.

They shook hands, Pollard leading Mahan past the older woman's desk to reach his private office. There was nothing on his desk except a blotter and three neatly lined-up pencils, but a row of filing cabinets against the room's north wall suggested Pollard was a busy man with wide responsibilities.

Like dumping DRS employees who'd caused problems in the field and left a bad taste in his mouth.

Pollard sat down behind the desk, half sinking out of sight, while Mahan took the usual uncomfortable seat reserved for visitors. He thanked Pollard for seeing him, then got right into it.

"I had a feeling on the phone, when I described the case I'm working on, that something might have rung a bell with you."

"There was a certain...resonance," Pollard confirmed with visible reluctance. "Nothing I can prove, mind you—nothing that would support a charge of any kind. If pressed, it might even result in slander charges or an accusation of discrimination. When religion gets involved...well, things get *sticky* sometimes."

"Understood," Mahan replied. "But at the same time, if you find yourself aware of anything—and I mean *anything*—that might prevent more heinous crimes from happening, I'd say you have an obligation to speak up."

Pollard was nodding now. "After we spoke long-distance, I consulted with our legal counsel here, and he agrees...up to a point. He's authorized sharing of information from our personnel files, but I can't and won't claim any knowledge of whatever acts a given ex-employee may have contemplated or committed after separation from the DRS."

"And no one could expect you to. If you'd prefer a court subpoena—"

"No, no!" Pollard raised both hands to silence Mahan. "I... we...don't wish to become involved in anything like that."

"Just two guys talking, then," said Mahan. "If it leads to nothing, there's no reason anyone should know we had this conversation. If it helps to catch a killer, I'd leave you and your superiors to judge if you want any credit for assisting law enforcement."

"We're agreed, then," Pollard said, trying to act relaxed. "There *was* one individual employed with us whose curious activities produced complaints from half a dozen farmers he approached with offers for their surplus livestock."

"By 'curious activities,' what do you mean, exactly?"

"As I understand, he would present himself to subjects normally, converse with them a while, then veer off into talk about the Bible, sacrificial offerings, that sort of thing. If six complained, my guess would be at least two or three times that number let it pass."

"When you say sacrificial offerings…"

"To God, apparently. Things out of the Old Testament, pleasing the Lord with blood and burning flesh, that sort of thing."

"Meaning the sacrifice of animals?"

Pollard blinked twice at that, his cheeks blanching. "I had no reason to suspect a more…extreme…interpretation."

"No. Why would you? But you fired him?"

"Not immediately. He was cautioned to remember that he served the U.S. government and private interjections of a personal nature, whatever those might be, were…ill advised."

"But he kept at it."

"As you say. If anything, the admonition seemed to *goad* him. After three more protests, two of them in writing, I dismissed him."

"And this fella's name was…?"

"Simon Cain. I'm authorized to let you see his personnel file, although not to copy or remove it from the building."

"Fair enough."

Pollard got up, moved to one of his filing cabinets, extracting a Manila folder and returning with it to the desk. Before he passed it over, he told Mahan, "As you'll see, he was the last man I'd expect to cause this sort of problem on the job."

"Because...?"

"He was a certified war hero, decorated for his gallantry in France and wounded in combat. If anyone was capable of understanding *duty*, I'd have said that man was Simon Cain."

"And yet."

Pollard was nodding. "Now I have to wonder whether something happened to him over there. Something no one could see unless he chose to let it show."

***

"A war hero?" Rose's expression was beyond surprise, verging on shock. "That can't be right."

"I saw the file," Mahan confirmed. "There's no mistake. He came home with a load of army decorations: the Victory Medal with Citation Star, plus Battle Clasps for three major campaigns in France, a Distinguished Service Medal and a Croix de Guerre the French awarded to him. He was shelled and gassed, finally sent back home for rehabilitation from the Veterans Bureau before the armistice."

"How badly was he hurt?"

"I can't access hospital files without a court order, and that's not happening."

"I mean, if he was crippled up and couldn't get around too well..."

"I *did* ask that. No disability on record with the DRS, and he was fit enough to drive around the district meeting farmers, buying cattle."

"And his name's really Cain?"

Mahan nodded. "It took a minute for me, but it linked up to that verse from Genesis."

"Like leaving you a clue."

"Maybe."

"This Mr. Pollard has no idea where he is?"

"No forwarding address required from people getting fired, unless they're owed a final paycheck. Cain took his with him and he hasn't been in contact with the DRS since then."

"Which was…?"

"September of last year," Mahan replied.

"About the time your killings started down in Texas."

"Pretty close."

"So, getting canned might've pushed him over the edge."

"If Cain's the guy. We won't know that for sure until we track him down somehow."

"You think that's even possible? He could have changed his name a dozen times by now, switched cars between one bunch of killings and the next. Was there a picture of him in the file?"

"A black-and-white from when they hired him. Looks like every third or fourth man passing on the street. Description with it says brown hair, brown eyes. The measured him at six foot one, one hundred eighty pounds, which could be up or down by now."

"Not much to go on," Rose observed.

"Unless he's dumb enough to use his given name sometimes while traveling around."

"And how would you trace that?"

"If I was still a Ranger, I could try to look up traffic tickets, auto sales, maybe hotel records, but that would take an operation on the scale of Hoover's FBI."

"And what about your agent friend?"

"I'll pass this on, but he was crystal-clear about not diving any deeper into it without some federal law to hang his hat on."

"Well, whoever's doing all of this, we may know where he was while we were driving back here yesterday."

"Want to explain that?"

"It was on the radio, not much, while you were at your meeting. Just a snippet out of Springfield, Colorado, wherever that is."

"What did it say?"

"Two women murdered. Newsman called them 'ladies of the evening.' Said that they were stabbed all over, one left with a rosary stuffed in her mouth."

***

Once Rose had filled him in, Mahan descended to the hotel lobby's pay phone booth. He asked the operator for two numbers—the Springfield Police Department's and the Baca County Sheriff's—wrote them down, then started feeding coins into the box mounted before him.

Colorado was on Mountain Standard Time, an hour earlier than Kansas, most of the Midwest, and portions of the South from Canada down to the Gulf of Mexico. He caught a Springfield homicide detective named Flannery on his way to lunch and none too pleased about the interruption, but he stuck around at mention of the Texas Rangers and a possible connection to his city's recent murders.

"What's your name again?" the faceless stranger asked.

Mahan repeated it and tacked on his badge number.

"And you think you've got a lead on what went down here yesterday?"

"I might. It's not identical to what I'm working on, but if I'm hearing right about religious symbolism in the case…"

"What *are* you working on?" Flannery asked.

"A string of murders starting late last year, spread out from Texas up to Kansas. Started out with family massacres on isolated farms, then shifted to an automatic weapon being used against a homeless caravan in Logan County, not so far from you. The count is up to thirty-two victims so far."

"I heard about that thing with the machine gun or whatever," Flannery admitted. "I can tell you that it's nothing like our stabbings here."

"In prior crimes, the man I'm looking for used knives as well firearms, cutting throats and mutilating corpses."

"Mm. And the religious angle?"

"I can't swear it's accurate, but on the news we're getting here, it claims one of your victims had a rosary inserted in her mouth."

"Let's say that's possible. So, what?"

"At least two of the cases I'm pursuing have presented something similar. In one, the killer backtracked to a scene after the bodies were removed, carving a cross and reference to scripture on the front door of a farmhouse. In the Logan County deal, two kids were crucified against one of the shot-up cars."

"Jesus! We don't have anything like that. I'll tell you off the record that our victims here were hookers, both with multiple arrests and fines. Our coroner says they were cut up separately, three or four hours apart on the same night, then left in bed together at a flophouse off Hickory Avenue. One guy behind it, fairly strong to carry 'em upstairs, but they were on the skinny side for my taste. Anything like that on your list?"

"Not so far."

"You said you're looking for somebody?"

"That may be a longshot," Mahan said. "There's nothing I could charge him with so far, but he was fired from Drought Relief last year for spouting gospel on the job, when he was sent to buy up cattle."

"Crazy talk?"

"Unwelcome, at the very least, and farmers out this way tend to be Christian types."

"On Sunday, anyhow," said Flannery. "They beefed about him to the agency?"

"Enough to get him warned one time, then booted when he kept it up."

"You got a name for me?"

"Employment record has him down as Simon Cain, age thirty-five, brown over brown, six-one, one-eighty. No address on file since he got canned."

"I'll run it through the system here. If I come up with anything or need to ask you something else, where can I reach you?"

"Kansas City now, but on the move. There's no point calling Texas, since they've got me on detached assignment."

Covering his tracks.

"Okay, then. Call me back sometime, the next two or three days, and sooner if you get a solid lead. It may be nothing, but—"

"It might."

"Who knows?"

"I hear you," Mahan said, and cut the link.

13

Colby, Kansas

"Simon Cain? Can that be you?"

The soldier paused, half of a corned beef sandwich inches from his lips and turned to face the owner of the voice that had distracted him. The Kopp's drugstore lunch counter did a decent business, but he still had stools open on either side of him.

He didn't recognize the man who'd spoken at first glance, but it came to him soon enough. His memory was sharp and clear—sometimes too much so for his liking.

"Dave Randall?"

"It *is* you! Maybe you remember that I go by 'Corky'?"

"Right."

Randall sat to Cain's left, uninvited, nudging him with an elbow. "What are the odds, us meeting up like this? Last time I saw you it was…where, again? In Tulsa?"

"Broken Arrow, south of Tulsa."

"Sure. I've got it now."

"And here we are," Cain offered, noncommittally.

"A wild coincidence," said Randall, reaching for a menu from the counter's rack. "And after yesterday, on top of everything."

Cain felt the short hairs stirring on his nape. "What happened yesterday, Corky?"

"Funniest thing." He flagged the waitress, ordered ham and Swiss on rye, potato chips and root beer back. "Do you remember Pollard?"

Cain repeated the surname, making a face as if it puzzled him, but he remembered Jacob Pollard very well indeed. The man, albeit inadvertently, had liberated him for full-time service to the Lord of Hosts.

"Sure, sure. You had that little problem with him toward the end, there?"

"Ah. Our parting of the ways."

"I never heard what that was all about," said Randall, probing.

"Disagreement over policy," Cain told him. "We agreed to disagree. No damage done."

"I guess not. From the look of you, you've done all right."

"I'm getting by."

"It's funny, though."

"What is?" Becoming irritated now, Cain took a bite out of his sandwich to distract himself.

"Well, he's calling around to us guys in the field. I'm still with DRS, you know?"

"It suits you, Corky. Calling about what?"

"See, that's the funny part. About *you*, buddy."

"I don't follow you." A sour feeling had begun in Cain's stomach. He fought it down and glommed another mouthful of his lunch, pretending to enjoy it now.

"Well, you know Pollard. Plays his cards close to the vest and don't share much around. But he's been calling people in the field—"

"You said that."

"Right. And asking if they've seen you lately. Anyhow, he asked *me* that. I can't remember when he called me last, then yesterday, our of the blue, bingo!"

"Not sure I follow you," Cain said, but thought he might be starting to.

"Somebody reached out to him. He was acting cagey, but I think it must've been a cop, something like that."

"Reached out?"

"Trying to find you, Sy. He wouldn't tell me *why*, of course, but if I had to judge his mood, I'd say he seemed a trifle tense, you know? Now, one day later, here you are. What are the odds?"

"I'd call them astronomical." A pause, hoping he didn't sound too interested, then he asked, "Was that the whole message?"

"In a nutshell."

"He left no word for me directly, if we happened to meet up?"

"I guess he thought it was a long-shot, like you say. The odds are astrological."

"But here we are."

"It's freaky, right?"

"That sums it up."

The waitress came with Randall's lunch and Cain told her to put it on his bill.

"Hey, thanks, Sy. You don't have to—"

"It's my pleasure."

Cain switched subjects, asking Randall what brought him to Colby, seat of Thomas County in the northwest corner of the state.

"Buying up cattle, sending 'em to slaughter, same as always.

Sometimes feels like I could make more as a butcher, but I never learned the trade. The cuts all sound alike to me, you know?"

"It takes specific education."

"Anyway, I'm covered under Civil Service, which your butchers ain't. You gotta love that job security in times like these." Randall's brain finally caught up with his mouth. "Oh, hey…I didn't mean…"

"Forget it. That book's closed, as far as I'm concerned."

"Okay. I talk too much sometimes. Forget to think ahead."

"It happens to the best of us."

They finished up their meals with small talk on the side, Cain slowing down to pace Randall. When they were done, he paid the bill and tipped the waitress using cash he'd taken from the whores in Sterling, after sacrificing them. He couldn't say if what he spent had come from Nancy's purse or Sarah's, but it made no difference to him, much less to them.

As they were leaving, Cain asked Randall, "How about a beer? I know a place nearby, McDougal's. Normally it's quiet, this time of the day."

"You drink beer now? I thought you were teetotal."

"People change. I've learned to do all kinds of things."

"How close is this McDougal's, Sy? I'm walking and—"

"My car's right over there," Cain said.

"No kidding?" Randall's eyes widened as he checked out the Packard Twelve. "You *must* be doing good."

"Pollard did me a favor, after all."

"I guess so. What a ride!"

Cain keyed open the Packard's curbside door and walked around to enter on the driver's side, saying, "Hop in, Corky. This won't take long."

***

Oakley, Kansas

"Welcome back! Can't stay away, I guess?"

Same goateed clerk behind the counter, with the same leer when he glanced at Rose, likely thinking how sly he was.

Mahan tried not to sound sour as he answered back, "A good thing goes a long way."

That puzzled the clerk, as he'd intended, but the guy wasn't a deep thinker. Switching gears, he said, "We've got a cabin with two beds available, no roller, if you want to double up. It's just a quarter more."

Rose nodded, kept her eyes averted from the clerk. Mahan replied, "We'll take it."

It had been a tossup coming back to Oakley from K.C., another long day on the road, but Logan County was the last place where their target—maybe Simon Cain, and maybe not—had made a major splash. Sterling, in Colorado, was two hundred twenty miles to the northwest, call it six more hours in the Ford and landing in the neighborhood of midnight when the killer was most likely gone by now.

After they'd inked the register, Mahan inquired about the office phone number, saying somebody might try reaching out to him "from work." He wrote it down, then used the public booth outside to leave Jacob Pollard the tip on where he could be reached.

Another longshot, but one of them paid off every now and then.

Their cabin, number seven, had two single beds, the only difference from where they'd stayed last time. Another Remington was mounted on the wall between those beds, this one called "Trooper on the Plains," showing a cavalryman with a bushy mustache and crossed bandoliers standing at east beside a weary-looking dapple gray.

"You think they got a discount on these prints?" Rose asked.

"I think they got a discount all the way around," Mahan replied.

Still, he had no complaints about the cabin's cleanliness and figured they could spend a few days there if necessary, hoping for a lead from Pollard back in Kansas City. Mahan frankly didn't put much store in that, but there were times during a manhunt when the best thing you could do was hunker down and bide your time. Sad as it was, he'd learned to follow killers by the trail of bodies in their wake.

They knew the nearby diners well enough, selected one at random, and got back into the Model A, rolling three-quarters of a mile westward on Highway 40. There was still room in its off-road parking lot, between a bulky Mack Truck and a Model T roadster that had seen better days since it debuted in 1926.

Inside, they got the last booth, leaving two stools at the counter for whoever turned up later. Mahan sat facing the door, conscious of the Smith and Wesson tucked under his jacket, pressing up against his spine. A waitress pushing forty brought them menus, filling up both coffee mugs and telling then she'd be back in a minute.

That stretched into ten before she circled back around with pad in hand, taking their orders for the porkchop special, mashed potatoes, mushroom gravy, and a buttermilk biscuit. Rose kept her voice down when they were alone once more, asking, "Do you think he's still around here somewhere?"

Mahan had his doubts and said so. "I wish we had a better

lead, but Colorado doesn't feel right?"

"Even with…those women?"

"If he did that—and I grant you that he might have—it's another break from his routine. Half of the state's included in the Dust Bowl, where he likes to prowl, but why not hit another farm? It strikes me as a hasty thing, someone fixing to leave and deciding to leave a reminder but something that wouldn't look much like the others."

"Just threw them away."

"He's beyond normal feelings at this point, whoever he is."

"But you still think it's Cain?"

"Let's say I *hope* it is. If not, we gained nothing at all by driving to K.C. and back."

"Do you expect to hear from Mr. Pollard."

Mahan held his answer while their meals arrived, the waitress moving out of earshot. "Fifty-fifty," he replied, "if he hears anything back from his people scattered far and wide. I have no doubt his boss would like to bury it and wish it all away."

"So many lives, and they're concerned about their petty reputations?"

"It's a knee-jerk human quality. Look out for Number One."

"It's wrong."

"You're preaching to the choir, Rose. But you don't spend any length of time behind a badge without discovering how people think and act."

"Bad people."

"I gave up on judging if there's no law being broken. Even then, something like drinking during Prohibition or a little gambling now and then, trying to legislate morality just spreads corruption and creates more problems than it solves."

"My parents didn't hold with liquor."

"And more power to them. I've seen drinking cause no end of grief, believe me. On the other hand, after America supposedly went 'dry' in 1920, known saloons quadrupled in Fort Worth and Dallas, neighborhoods like Hell's Half-Acre and Frogtown. You didn't have to ask a cabbie for directions. Walk down any street and watch the cops lined up outside for payoffs and free drinks."

"Shameful."

"And human. Now, we've got a loony running wild, apparently hyped up on his interpretation of the Bible, likely thinking that he gets his marching orders from Upstairs."

"He's wrong."

Mahan didn't respond to that. He'd read enough scripture over the years to know its authors had been fans of slavery and random wars that led to "ripping up" of pregnant women, dashing babies to the stony ground, and raiding villages to capture virgin "wives." The Lord Himself had given Pharaoh three chances to free Israeli captives, then came back and personally hardened Pharaoh's heart each time, after he had decided to comply, and slaughtered all of Egypt's first-born as a lesson.

Teaching what? That the Almighty could demand obedience, receive it three times over, and then dish out punishment regardless?

Most anyone could find a message in the Good Book, telling them to scurry off in this or that direction, maybe spreading charity or burning hapless women at the stake for being "witches," based on warts or spiteful rumors.

Rose had her opinions, which might never mesh with his, and that was fine.

For now, they had a common goal, and after that…

"All done?" he asked, noting her empty plate.

"I'm getting tired."

"Let's turn in, then. If you don't mind, I'll take the bed next to the door."

***

Kansas Highway 40, Eastbound

It hadn't taken Cain much time to realize that Corky Randall had no further useful information to impart.

They'd never made it to McDougal's bar, which to the best of Cain's personal knowledge was a myth. Two hard blows with the Mark I trench knife's knuckleduster shattered both of Randall's cheekbones but still left him capable of speaking between ragged sobs, while drooling blood and snot. He swore to Christ that he knew nothing more about why Jacob Pollard was belatedly sniffing around on Cain's trail, and when they'd exhausted that topic, Cain cut his throat from ear to ear, leaving his body in a butcher shop's back-alley trash bin.

Driving east toward Kansas City, Cain marveled again at Colby and surrounding Thomas County, both with posted highway signs that told all comers they were "GROWING STRONG" despite nature's upheavals and the manmade Great Depression. Colby covered less than four square miles but claimed its population of some twenty-one hundred inhabitants had grown by 93 percent since 1920s census. Thomas County was a good deal larger, better than one thousand square miles, but its headcount lagged behind the county seat's, increased by only 33 percent between decennial assessments. Beyond that, most observers found the

Kansas population slipping, beaten farmers taking their cue from a small army of hobos, heading west.

The drive from Colby to K.C. spanned three hundred seventy miles—around four hours minus gas stops if he could unleash the Packard to its limit—but the problem came from towns along the route, ranging from Oakley and WaKeeney to Salina and Topeka. In these blighted times, some of the smaller settlements survived on filling stations, greasy spoons and speed traps run be lawmen who made more from bilking travelers than from their monthly salaries. He used discretion, kept his Army .45 beneath a folded newspaper beside him, and decided he would deal with any obstacles as they arose.

His plan, when he arrived in Kansas City, was simplicity itself. Lay hands on Jacob Pollard, squeeze the little rat until he spilled his guts—both figuratively speaking and in other ways—to find out who was asking after Cain and why.

It might be nothing, or it could foretell the End of Days.

In either case, the soldier was prepared.

***

Oakley, Kansas

Mahan had no reason to believe they'd come under attack that night, but lying in his bed nearest the cabin's door, already double-locked and with the room's lone chair braced underneath the knob, he kept his Smith & Wesson Magnum close at hand.

Rose showered while he listened to the radio, scanning the dial for news and finding none that was related to their quest. When she'd emerged and gone to bed, he shaved, used the commode, and came back, slipping off his trousers only when he'd killed the last lamp burning.

"Maybe we'll hear something in the morning," Rose said.

"It could happen," he agreed, not feeling it too likely overall.

"Goodnight, then."

" 'Night."

From the tenor of her breathing, Rose appeared to fall asleep almost at once. It took Mahan the best part of an hour, drifting off. It was not late according to his normal standard, but an early start still seemed important for some reason that he couldn't put his finger on.

Lying awake, his right hand draped over the Magnum's grip, he wondered about Rose's state of mind, how she was bearing up behind the brave front she presented and how long she could continue on their aimless trek pursuing justice or revenge.

Since the eradication of his family in Texas, both goals seemed identical to Mahan.

If he found the killer and somehow contrived to capture him alive, his vigilante action might be used by the defense at trial. That likely wouldn't get the bastard far in Texas, where associated bankers printed posters reading "WANTED DEAD" for members of the Barrow gang. Granted, an outcry from the press had forced the posters' authors to go back and add a small-print "OR ALIVE" under the glaring sixty-point headline, but finally it hadn't mattered either way, since Captain Hamer's posse never planned on taking any prisoners.

Conversely, if Mahan identified the murderer and executed him "in self-defense," he might be charged with homicide unless he pulled it off back home in Texas, where the public mood, together with his record as a Ranger, ought to get him off the hook.

Lying wide-awake in darkness, Mahan wished he had a beer or six to lull his agitation, but he knew that getting soused would only leave him with a hangover tomorrow, slowing his reflexes while potentially endangering Rose and himself.

Whatever happened next, over the days to come, he had assumed the burden of protecting her and Mahan was committed not to fail, as bitter instinct told him he had failed his family.

Misguided guilt, perhaps, but none the less painful.

And he supposed that it could only be absolved by spilling blood.

If that included *his* blood with the killer's—whether he was Simon Cain the war hero or someone else unknown—it made no difference. Forgiveness called for sacrifice, and even then it still might be impossible.

But if the murderer escaped, it would not be for lack of Mahan's effort.

He would gladly die in that pursuit, if it meant finishing the man who'd left his life in ruins.

And with that thought foremost in his mind, Mahan slipped into darkness with the sound of his alarm clock tick-tock-ticking in his ears.

14

Kansas City, Kansas

Jacob Pollard left his office on State Avenue the best part of an hour late, which had become his usual departure time over the past eleven months. With no one waiting for him at his small apartment north of Wilson Boulevard, there was no hurry getting home and nothing to distract him from the trouble nagging him of late.

Murders, for God's sake, and he'd gone out on a limb to offer up the only suspect he could think of, with permission from his supervisor, making calls around his district to find out if any other DRS agents had seen or heard from Simon Cain since he was separated from the service. So far, the replies were negative, and Pollard hoped they'd stay that way. What-ever Cain had done, whatever he had coming to him, Pollard wanted no part of it adding serious demerits to his file.

The Texas Ranger, Mahan, wasn't letting go of course. He'd called back just today, leaving his contact information for some tourist court in western Kansas, seeking any further information Pollard might obtain as it came dribbling in.

Pollard had played along, scribbled his name, location and a phone number on a scrap of paper from his desk and stashed it in a trouser pocket with his spare change, while explaining that he'd heard nothing so far and wasn't likely to.

It was a warm late afternoon, despite a breeze that wafted from the Kansas River, also widely known as "Kaw" from its name in an ancient tribal dialect. He didn't need a topcoat, hadn't even brought one in today from home. His gold pince-nez was tucked into a vest pocket, the leather briefcase in his left hand heavy with various reports he planned to scrutinize after his normal dinner at Luigi's, were spaghetti *alla carbonara* had become his usual, preceded by a bowl of minestrone soup, together with a glass or two of rosé to relax after his day.

More wine waiting at home, and lately Pollard had begun to wonder if he had a drinking problem, but if so, it hadn't interfered with his performance of his job as yet, so who cared anyway?

Not Charlotte, who had blamed him for their failure to have children, spending more time at the office than he did at home, and finally decided there was no saving their eight-year marriage. By the time it came to that, Pollard could dredge up no good reason to object and signed the papers, giving her their small house in the Fairfax District on Goose Island's river bend and moving to a three-room walkup closer to his job.

Ironically, the Great Depression helped him out with alimony, capping it at thirty dollars monthly from his salary since Charlotte kept the house and could dispose of it at will. He'd kept the Model T and nearly counted himself lucky in the end.

Nearly.

He missed companionship, of course, but even that was fading in the stretch.

The federal building had no watchman on its parking lot, a lapse that Pollard had remarked on more than once without reply from his superiors. Guards weren't considered necessary and he couldn't argue with that view, since there had never been an incident so far. Despite the FBI's "crime war," the massacre at Union Station on the far side of the river two years earlier, Pollard was unaware of any threats against his agency or the tall structure where he worked five days per week.

Pollard was fishing in the right-hand pocket of his trousers for his car key when a man rose from concealment on the Model T's far side. He was taller than Pollard but the district supervisor probably would not have recognized him if he hadn't opened Simon Cain's employment file so recently.

"Mr. Pollard," said the man he'd hoped to never see again. Expecting him.

Trying to keep his face deadpan, Pollard replied, "Are we acquainted, sir?"

"I hate to think that you've forgotten me," Cain said, and smiled.

"I'm sure I don't know what you mean." His hands were trembling now, Pollard hoping his briefcase and the key would help disguise their tremor.

"Is that how you want to play it?" Cain was moving toward him, circling around the Ford's rear bumper. "Putting on an act?"

"What do you want?"

"A little chat. It won't take long."

A brass-bound fist hurtled toward Pollard's face and blotted out the world.

***

Oakley, Kansas

There wasn't much Mahan could do without more information coming in—either a tip from Pollard in K.C. or, God forbid, another massacre. So, after breakfast, when Rose asked if she could see his other guns, he cautiously agreed and drove the Model A south along Highway 83 until they found a long-abandoned farm and pulled in there, circling around behind its sagging barn, well out of sight.

That done, he raised the backseat's hinged cushion and started hauling out the rest of his accumulated arsenal, laying the guns out on a blanket spread along the Ford's hood, from its windshield to the radiator cap.

He started small, with a Colt Detective Special, the first "snub-nose" revolver with a barrel just two inches long, the whole thing measuring six inches and three-quarters, weighing just under two pounds. Unlike his Smith & Wesson, it fired only .38 Special rounds and was intended for concealment by plainclothes detectives, hence its brand name.

"Why does it have rubber bands around the grip?" Rose asked.

The buttstock is a little small for some hands," Mahan said. "Also, the rubber helps with gripping when you have to pull it in a hurry. If you need to drop it somewhere, there's the added benefit of hiding fingerprints."

"Unless you've touched the metal bits."

"That's true, but oil and powder residue obscure more prints after a weapon's fired than most cops want you to believe."

"Good news for criminals, I guess."

His next piece was a Winchester Model 1892 lever-action rifle, a descendant of the company's popular Models 1873 and 1886. Chambered for .44-40 Winchester rounds, it benefited cowboys and ranchers by feeding the same ammunition they commonly loaded in handguns, eliminating any need for carrying diverse rounds and perhaps confusing them in an emergency.

The rifle measured 49.21 inches from its muzzle to the butt plate of its walnut stock, with 24.41 inches being blue steel barrel. It weighed 9.92 pounds unloaded and held twelve rounds in the tubular magazine under its barrel. A skilled shooter could empty those twelve shots within a minute, sending fifteen-gram bullets out to a hundred yards at one thousand feet per second.

"Papa had a Winchester, older than this," Rose said. "Called it the Yellow Boy."

"The Model 1866," Mahan replied, "named for the bronze and brass alloy they used for its receiver."

"He went out hunting one time and fell somehow. Broke off the best part of its stock and never got around to fixing it."

"They're sturdy, but it happens sometimes," he agreed.

The next gun on display, another Winchester, was the company's Model 1912 pump-action shotgun, featuring an internal hammer and external tube magazine that matched Mahan's rifle. Introduced as the "perfect repeater," it had set the standard for pump-action scatterguns since then. Twelve-gauge shells were loaded underneath the gun, empties ejected to the right. Its magazine held five, plus one more in the chamber if a shooter kept the safety on until he planned on killing something—or someone.

Mahan's shotgun weighed eight pounds and measured 39.25 inches overall, its barrel twenty inches long. That cut effective range for hunting wildlife but allowed a better spread for double-aught buckshot, nine pellets to a shell, with each one the size of a .33-caliber bullet. No man could stand against it at close range, and even one pellet could kill if it pierced any vital organs.

"Papa had a lever-action," Rose observed. "It looked more like your rifle, only shorter."

"That would be the Model 1887. Obsolete some people call it nowadays, but I've seen plenty of them working fine."

"He never got a chance to use it when it counted."

"Rifles always have the farther reach."

He'd saved the best for last, borrowed with no intention of returning it when he'd retired to hunt the slayer of his family, suspecting that he might need more firepower than a Ranger on his own normally carried.

"Oh, my!" Rose said, as he revealed his pride and joy.

The grand finale was a Thompson submachine gun, Model 1921A, designed as a "trench broom" for the Great War but it had entered production too late to see battle. Since Prohibition's onset it was widely known as the "Tommy gun," "chopper," or the "Chicago typewriter," most infamous for its employment during 1929's St. Valentine's Day massacre.

The Thompson weight 10.8 pounds empty and measured 33.7 inches from its stubby muzzle to its detachable stock's butt plate, with a walnut pistol grip mounted beneath its finned 10.52-inch barrel. It fired the same .45 ACP rounds as Colt's M1911 pistol, cycling full-auto rounds at six hundred per minute, spreading death out to 164 yards with a muzzle velocity of 935 feet per second.

Shooters couldn't really fire six hundred rounds per minute, naturally, since the Thompson fed its rounds from "stick" magazines holding twenty rounds each, or hand-wound drums loaded with fifty or one hundred cartridges apiece. Civilian sales were commonplace until the 1934 National Firearms Act required registration and payment of a $200 transfer tax on each sale, but those with ready cash on hand could still acquire a Tommy gun over the counter at their local sporting goods emporium—or, if they operated on the shady side, from armorers who served the underworld.

"I've heard of these but only seen them in the newsreels," Rose said. "Johnny Dillinger and such."

"He liked 'em pretty well," Mahan agreed. They hadn't saved Dillinger, though, shot down last summer in Chicago as he left a movie with a woman who had sold him out.

"Do you suppose I could hold onto this one?" she asked, pointing to the Colt Detective Special.

Mahan considered it. Asked, "Have you ever handled a revolver?"

"Not yet."

"All right. Let me put the rest of these away, then we can try some target practice in the barn."

"You have enough spare ammunition?"

"Not a problem," Mahan said. "I came loaded for bear."

***

Kansas City, Kansas

Jacob Pollard didn't have a clue where he'd been taken when he regained consciousness, head throbbing mercilessly dried blood caking on his face. He blinked and looked around, discovered he was lying on the ground beside his own Ford Model T. Some thirty yards in front of him, a river that he took to be the Kansas rushed along below a shallow bluff.

Still somewhere in or near the city, then, but as to where…

"Awake, are we?" the voice of his abductor asked, as dusty shoes and trouser legs came into view.

Despite the brutal flare of pain it caused inside his skull, Pollard rolled back against the Ford's rear wheel, the driver's side he realized, and peered up at the man who had attacked him leaving work. Trying to keep up a façade of ignorance and thereby save himself, he asked, "Who are you? What's this all about?"

"Still play-acting," said Simon Cain. "I hoped you'd have more sense than that and make it easy on yourself."

"I don't know what—"

"Enough!" Cain raged at him. He reached into the right-hand pocket of his coat, pulled out a piece of colored paper Pollard recognized at once, feeling his heart sink at the sight of it.

"I see you know what this is, *Mister* Pollard. I recognize your handwriting from my dismissal notice, but I'll read it for you, just in case you want to keep on playing dumb."

Pollard said nothing, waited while Cain raised the note he'd scrawled while on the telephone that morning, and began to read aloud. "Wallace Mahan. Sunflower Tourist Court, Oakley. And you've jotted down a phone number. That's Oakley, Kansas, I assume? In Logan County, slopping over into Gove and Thomas?"

Pollard thought it best to offer no reply.

"Funny," his kidnapper pressed on. "I was in Logan County not too long ago, doing a spot of work. You may have heard about it. Thirteen filthy hobos went to their reward."

Pollard couldn't silence the small moan arising in his throat.

"I see you know me now," Cain said. "Can we dispense with any more tomfoolery? Who is this Mahan character? What does he want from you and I?"

Pollard decided he had precious little left to lose, a since of liberation coming over him. "Not me," he answered back. "Mahan's a Texas Ranger hunting you for all the blood you've spilled."

"A Ranger in Kansas? He must be lost. I'm betting that's not legal."

"Seems to be a trend these days. Ask Clyde Barrow and Bonnie Parker."

"You equate me with that scum?"

Cain took a short step forward, drew his right foot back, and booted Pollard in the gut. Pollard heaved up the remnants of his lunch, then spat a few times, clearing bile out of his mouth. His voice was feeble as he said, "And you're a coward, as expected."

Cain crouched in front of him, reached back and drew something he'd tucked under his belt. The knuckleduster that he'd used on Pollard looked familiar, but the injured man now saw it formed the handle of a knife, its blade long, black, and double-edged.

"You have no inkling what I am," Cain said, "much less what I'm becoming. If you have the brains Our Maker gave a gnat, you'll tell me everything you know about this Ranger far from home. Do that, and I'll release you quickly. More than you deserve."

"You have it all right there," said Pollard, nodding toward the note in Cain's left hand.

"Not all. I need to know exactly what you told him, what he knows, whether you have another contact with him planned."

"Go straight to Hell!" Pollard replied.

"You first," Cain said.

And leaning close, he went to work.

***

Oakley, Kansas

Mahan was pleased with Rose's handling of the Colt snub-nose, especially for someone who had never previously fired a pistol. After three rounds she could hit the two-by-four he'd chosen as her target, with a bullseye penciled on the warped and faded plank. Three more shots, and she put one in the ring, the other two both close enough to count as crippling wounds if it had been a man.

The second six, she landed four inside the kill zone from a range Mahan had designated as the short Colt's favored showdown range.

By then, their ears were ringing. He'd neglected buying cotton and announced that they should get some on their way to celebrate with dinner. Lawmen didn't walk around with cotton in their ears all day, expecting rude surprises on their beats, but more of them were taking wise precautions on the practice firing range these days.

Deaf cops weren't much use on the street.

They chose a steakhouse on South Freeman Avenue, just north of Highway 40, ordering two T-bones, baked potatoes and side salads. While they waited for their food, both sipping Coca-Colas, Rose asked Mahan, "So, I did okay?"

"You did fine," he replied. "I wouldn't say you're ready for a faceoff with our guy, but no one ever really is until it happens."

"You weren't ready, then? The first time?"

Rose assumed there had been more than one, and she was right. While Mahan couldn't match Frank Hamer's count of fifty-three acknowledged kills, he'd put more than a dozen badmen in the ground.

"The first time," he recalled, "I'd just turned twenty-two. A gang of bandits had come up from Mexico and they were raising hell along the Rio Grande, in Brewster and Presidio Counties. Me and another Ranger twice my age, Todd Baker, got the order and we ran them down a few miles south of Marla, on a farm they'd occupied after they shot the family."

"Something like now," she said,

"But strictly money at the root of it."

"What did you do?"

"Todd called them out. They cussed us for a while, then made a break for it. We carried single-action Colts back then, and Yellow Boy Winchesters like your pa had. Six of them against the pair of us. All firing like there's no tomorrow."

"And?"

"For them, there wasn't."

"How'd you feel?"

"Relieved," said Mahan. "I've heard some guys claim it made them sick or cost them sleep. The only thing I can remember thinking, then or later, was 'They made the call. It's better them than us.' "

"I see that."

"No two people feel the same, I guess. Some Rangers, other cops I've known, would talk about it like a squirrel hunt, till you notice that they're drinking more and keeping to themselves. Others seem to enjoy it, but I always wondered whether they were working on the wrong side of the law.

Same thing with soldiers, in my limited experience. Some take to battle like a duck to water, others fall apart, but most land somewhere in between."

"I can't imagine it would bother me to shoot the man who killed my parents and my brother."

"Maybe not," said Mahan. "But if you can put it off or skip it altogether, don't feel cheated by it. If somebody else who's done it takes the weight, it's no reflection on yourself."

"But if I had to..."

"When the moment comes, you find out pretty quick."

"I guess."

"Best not to think about that too much in advance. It undercuts your nerve."

"My father would've tried to save us." There was moisture showing in her eyes now, but it didn't stop her forking up another bite of beef.

"Maybe he did," Mahan replied.

"How's that?"

"He couldn't stop the rifleman with what he had on hand, but I'd say he bought time for you to hide."

"I never thought of it that way."

"It couldn't hurt to try," he said, and turned back to demolishing his steak.

15

Kansas City, Kansas

After wringing Jacob Pollard dry of information, finishing him off, Cain dragged the gutted remnant to the river and delivered it for cleansing, watching as the current swept him off downstream and sucked him under, headed for its merger with the great Missouri, longest river on the continent of North America.

Wherever and whenever Pollard surfaced, if he ever did in fact, locals would have a grisly mystery to solve with no leads pointing back toward Simon Cain.

Not that it mattered any more.

His enemies had failed to stop him yet, because he was protected by the Lord, and no power on Earth could foil His plan.

Cain drove the dead man's Model T back to the spot where he had left his Packard Twelve, secure in a public parking lot along State Avenue. He made a cursory attempt at wiping down the Ford for fingerprints, mostly the steering wheel and door handles, but didn't waste a lot of time on it. From there, behind the Packard's wheel, he steered it back to Highway 40 and began the long drive west to Logan County.

Despite a sense of wasted time in starting off another drive across the state, three hundred fifty miles he'd covered once already over Highway 40, Cain felt no sense of frustration. He had offered up his future to Jehovah and would go where he was sent without complaint or any purpose of evasion. Somewhere, at the end of this road or another, he would find his enemy, eliminate the threat, then push on toward the culmination of his mission.

It would help, of course, if he could make another sacrifice along the way, but that decision was no longer his. Cain was convinced that God was setting his agenda, and if He required another trial of faith, so be it.

This Wallace Mahan interested him. He'd never heard the name before or suffered any interaction with the Texas Rangers during service with the DRS or afterward. He couldn't say how any Ranger might have linked him to the Lone Star sacrifices he'd performed, but that was something to be learned when he confronted Mahan in the flesh.

Even if Cain was forced to peel it from his bones in the pursuit or answers.

And the more the thought about that, urging on the Packard Twelve to greater speed while watching out for lawmen on the prowl, the more that idea pleased him.

It pleased him very much.

Cain tried the Packard's dashboard radio and found a station playing gospel music, picking up Mahalia Jackson singing "Hand Me Down My Silver Trumpet, Gabriel." Cain joined the harmony, his voice deep and mellifluous inside the speeding car.

If a passenger had been along to see Cain's smile, it would have made his blood run cold.

***

Oakley, Kansas

Mahan and Rose tried some variety for breakfast, visiting another diner for the first time. It was called Eileen's, but upon entering, they noted that the cook and the apparent owner, barking orders at two harried-looking waitresses, was a stout man of middle age wearing a sweat-stained paper cap over a wilted apron marked with grease stains.

"I hope that's not Eileen," Rose whispered through a smile.

"Smart money bets against it."

Mahan ordered coffee, black, while Rose opted for orange juice. From the menus labeled "BRAKEFAST," Mahan ordered two eggs fried with bacon, hash browns and rye toast. Rose went for something called a river omelet that he'd never heard of, oven-baked, including bacon, cheese, tomatoes, olives and mushrooms. When it arrived, Mahan wished that he'd tried one for himself, but found his serving ample and delicious on its own.

They took their time with breakfast, having nowhere in particular to go, nothing to do offhand. Mahan wasn't expecting any further leads from Jacob Pollard but had left the office number of their tourist court with the unhappy DRS director just in case. It wasn't totally impossible that someone on the government's payroll would happen onto Simon Cain, although Mahan supposed the odds of that were similar to those of finding a gold nugget lying in the middle of Main Street.

He thought about placing another call to Frank O'Neal in Dallas, but it felt like he'd already worn his welcome with the G-man perilously thin and didn't want to burn that bridge entirely through excessive pushiness. Beyond that, there was no one left for him to call and ask for help.

"A day off, then?" Rose asked.

"You read my mind. The only trouble is, I'm not sure what that feels like."

"You must've heard that saying about all work and no play."

"The trouble is, I've been a dull boy all my life," Mahan replied.

"I don't believe that for a second...Uncle Wally."

"Hey, now."

"Only joshing. Chasing bandits on the border, shootouts in the Wild West. If I look a little deeper into that, you might turn out to be a bona fide legend."

"Not even close. Most of the legends died with their boots on. We've got a couple left—Frank Hamer, Manny Gault, 'Lone Wolf' Gonzaullas—but they're running out of time. Those days are closing fast."

"We'll always need good lawmen," Rose replied.

"I'm not sure that applies to me these days."

"It doesn't matter whether you're retired or not," she said. "It's how you've lived your life, the things you've done. The things you're doing now."

"Like plotting murder with a girl who's half my daughter's age?"

"It isn't murder, putting down a mad dog. That's called self-defense."

"Remember that, will you," Mahan replied, "when someone slaps the cuffs on me?"

***

Kansas Highway 40

North of Ellsworth, seat of Ellsworth County, Cain imagined that a Motor Vehicle Inspector had been eyeballing the Packard Twelve, maybe trying to clock its speed, but the patrolman didn't swing around to follow him when Cain applied his brakes a bit, dropping from seventy to sixty miles per hour on the straightaway.

Maybe the cop had other business on his mind or simply didn't feel like chasing after vehicles he couldn't catch in his Ford Model B. In any case, deciding to ignore Cain made this afternoon his lucky day.

The .45 Colt riding close beside the stolen Packard's driver would have finished him in nothing flat and left another mystery unsolved in the Jayhawker State.

Cain knew a bit about the term "Jayhawker's" origins. Back in the 1850s, when the territory had been known as Bleeding Kansas due to strife surrounding slavery, Jayhawkers were free-soilers sworn to wipe out slave owners who they described as "Border Ruffians" or "Bushwhackers." Many Jayhawkers wrapped their boots in crimson leggings and were therefore known as "Red Legs." When the Civil War broke out in 1861, they'd formed guerilla bands and raided slave plantations, drawing retribution from the likes of Quantrill's Raiders that resulted in the Lawrence massacre of August 1863, leaving between one hundred sixty and one hundred ninety persons dead, depending who you asked, on which side of the Mason-Dixon Line.

Cain had mixed feelings when it came to talk about the

War Between the States. On the one hand, no one could deny the Holy Bible came down hard in the defense of slavery, except when God told Egypt's Pharaoh to release the Israelites. Conversely, abolitionists including many northern ministers had cherry-picked their way through scripture, citing verses they pretended were opposed to human bondage. One such, Henry Ward Beecher, a Congregationalist reverend whose sister wrote the novel *Uncle Tom's Cabin,* shipped muskets to fanatic Kansas Jayhawkers labeled as "Beecher's Bibles" while the border war was at its worst.

Cain didn't think much about slavery or black folks in the modern day. A pair of constitutional amendments made them citizens and granted them the right to vote during the postwar 1860s, but since then, states pledged to white supremacy had balanced those demands with Jim Crow laws, restrictive covenants in real estate zoning, and sundry barriers to suffrage that included poll taxes, white primaries, and tricked-up literacy tests, the Klan and lynch mobs standing by if all else failed.

None of that troubled Simon Cain. He operated on a higher plane, received his orders from the only Man of War who mattered in the universe. He would continue on the course that had been set for him until he triumphed or was slain and someone else stepped up to take his place.

In Oakley, he stopped at the first gas station on his route, bearing the sign of Humble Oil, though oilmen, in his personal experience, were anything but humble. Parking off to one side of the pumps Cain went inside, put on a phony smile, and asked directions to a tourist court called Sunflower. The sallow grease monkey knew where it was, another two miles down the road, and Cain made sure to thank him as he exited into the shadows of late afternoon.

Now all he had to do was locate Wallace Mahan and then figure out the best way to destroy him.

***

Rose finally persuaded Mahan to relax a bit and go to see a movie after lunch. The went to the Crystal Theatre on East Front Street for a double feature with Barbara Stanwyck as sharpshooter *Annie Oakley* (a local icon) and Edward G. Robinson spreading corruption in *Barbary Coast*. Before the films, they laughed at cartoons—"Betty Boop and Grampy," followed by "Little Black Sambo"—and watched a newsreel filled with marching Nazis overseas and G-men hunting remnants of the Barker-Karpis gang at home.

Their admission tickets cost a quarter each, while popcorn sold for a nickel per bag. Mahan determined to enjoy himself and managed it, despite misgivings and some nasty sidelong glances from the audience's older women, miffed at seeing him in company with an attractive female who appeared to be roughly one-third his age.

The men he noticed smiling at him all looked envious.

Emerging from the Crystal in late afternoon, the sunlight lanced their eyes at first, giving Mahan a vague idea of how Bela Lugosi was supposed to feel in *Dracula*. He hadn't shared the public passion for that tale of lurking bloodsuckers, nor *Frankenstein*, released the same year, since he'd hunted down too many living, breathing monsters on his job.

After a while, mayhem and derring-do lost their real-world appeal, except for criminals and certain trigger-happy cops who lived with one foot on each side of the dividing line.

He checked his watch, glanced up and down the street, then asked his unexpected date, "What now? Too full for supper, I suppose?"

"You're kidding, right?" Rose flashed a smile at Mahan. "I've been hungry since I got out of that rotten so-called hospital."

"Where do you put it?"

"I'm a growing girl, in case you hadn't noticed."

Mahan let that pass. He settled for, "We'd better get you fed then, so you don't wind up eating your pillow overnight."

"Ha-ha. Has anybody ever said you should be on the stage?"

"Only the last one out of town," Mahan replied.

That got a laugh that seemed more courteous than heart-felt, but he'd take whatever he could get. "What do you feel like having, then?"

"Seafood," she answered. "But I guess we're out of luck."

"One way to find out," Mahan said, and started scouting for a pay phone booth with a directory intact. Failing at that, he ducked into a butcher's shop with Rose trailing behind.

The shop's proprietor, a roly-poly walking advertisement for his trade, beamed at them, showing off a gold eyetooth as he inquired, "What can I do you for?"

"We're looking for a place that might serve decent sea-food," Mahan said. "Just passing through and staying at a tourist court, no kitchen, or I'd take some of that salmon off your hands."

"No problem, sir. I understand completely. You should make a run to Captain Jack's. They've got most anything, and steaks besides."

"Where might I find that?" Mahan queried.

"Five blocks, maybe six, due east of where we're standing. When you get to Geisler Avenue, turn left—that's north—and go another block or so. Can't miss the sign."

"Obliged."

"My pleasure. Come again, if you decide to stick around a while and get a stove."

They found the restaurant precisely as described, went in and let a smiling hostess seat them near the kitchen. Starting off with appetizers—crab cakes for Mahan, a shrimp cocktail for Rose—they moved on to a blackened catfish (his) and swordfish (hers).

"I never even heard of swordfish," Rose confided, when the waiter took their orders to the kitchen.

"Had a steak from one some years ago," Mahan allowed, "while I was working out of Corpus Christi on the Gulf. Not bad, as I recall."

"In for a penny, right?"

"That's what they say."

She frowned then. Said, "I mean to pay you back for all of this one day. Won't be tomorrow, but my I've got my mind made up."

"Forget about it," Mahan said. "We're in this thing together to the end."

16

Simon Cain had come away from grilling Jacob Pollard with a rough description of his enemy. He knew that Wallace Mahan was a white man in his early-to-mid fifties, graying hair, about six feet, close to one hundred ninety pounds.

Of that much he was reasonably sure, trusting in Pollard's mortal pain to make him speak the truth, although his guesswork as to height and weight might be inaccurate. Some people were no good at judging things like that, especially when they were bleeding out and screaming.

So, he made allowances.

As far as Cain knew, Texas Rangers were all white men, though they might have hired a few Hispanics since the Great War overseas, screening those applicants for size and attitude. Headlines told him that certain Rangers had been known to work outside of Texas, mostly hunting high-profile bank robbers, but he'd drawn a blank so far on why one of them would be tracking him.

Sure, Cain had executed seven sacrificial victims in the

Lone Star State, but even if those two raids had been linked, how would that lead a Ranger to interrogate a DRS director based in Kansas City?

Problems to be solved, but Cain would find the answers he required once he laid hands on Mahan and began to squeeze him dry. At some point in that process, all would be revealed.

The tourist court where his intended target was supposed to be residing, called the Sunflower, seemed fairly well kept up, at least from the outside. Its sign boasted the flower it was named for, rising roughly twenty feet above the parking lot, which had been swept sometime within the past couple of days. A maid was finishing her rounds, pushing a cart loaded with soiled linens in front of her, taking her time while counting down the tag end of her shift.

She wasn't bad looking, curvaceous even in her cheesy uniform and flats, but Cain no longer harbored any fascination for the female form. God had relieved him of his carnal lust.

Well, most of it.

Watching the layout from a corner, staying mostly out of sight, he'd seen the office manager and didn't like the look of him. His hairy chin made him resemble a cut-rate Lothario and even from a distance he had shifty eyes. Cain wouldn't trust him with a nickel, much less leaving private property under his care, but he supposed good men were hard to find for dead-end jobs waiting on tourists.

There was still an outside chance he might prove useful, but God's warrior hadn't worked out any details in his mind.

After his first drive past the Sunflower, Cain *had* phoned in check if Wallace Mahan was still staying at the tourist court. Things chance, and Cain had no wish to waste days and nights watching a place his adversary had abandoned prior to his arrival.

As expected, Mahan had supplied Cain's former DRS employer with the office number. From his personal experience at traveling, Cain knew few tourist courts provided telephones to paying guests, and those that did would have a manager or switchboard operator screening calls, recording bills down to the second, whether local or long-distance. When the shady clerk picked up, Cain asked if his friend Wallace Mahan might be registered and heard a lazy, "Yep. Sure is."

Phase One accomplished.

Next, Cain went in search of someplace he could lure Mahan for a private meeting, well away from prying eyes. He had a lie cooked up, spinning from his real-life experience with Corky Randall in Colby. He'd use a pseudonym, to be determined later, claiming that he was a DRS field agent who'd received a call from Jacob Pollard, seeking information on the exiled Simon Cain, and Pollard had provided Mahan's contact information to remove himself as middleman.

It was the sort of thing a coward like the DRS director might have done, if he were still alive.

Phase Two: Once he had found a place to drop the net on Mahan, Cain had phoned the Sunflower a second time and left a message for the man he sought, referring to an urgent message that required a meeting, giving the address, then having to repeat it while the clerk took notes, speaking the street number aloud. That done, he told Cain, "Okay, got it" and hung up.

Rude prick.

Phase Three took Cain back to the tourist court, pretending that he was a cop on stakeout for a wanted fugitive.

That wasn't so far-fetched, in fact, since he was under orders from the Lord to wipe out any hurdles that obstructed the completion of his mission.

Cain was watching when a dusty Model A pulled in from Highway 40, parking with its nose in toward the door of cabin number seven. When the driver exited, Cain thought he'd found his man, but then a teenage girl got out the other side, confusing him no end. The mismatched couple spoke a moment, then the man handed the key cabin's to his companion—daughter, wife he'd snatched out of a cradle, maybe some damned harlot off the streets—and turned back toward the office.

While the girl went on inside and shut the door behind her, Cain watched Mr. X talk to the manger, who nodded, fumbled underneath the counter, and retrieved a note he passed across. Mahan—it had to be him—asked a few more questions, but the clerk knew nothing more and simply shook his head until the Ranger left.

But who in Hades was the girl?

No matter.

Her appearance on the scene had given Cain a new, improved idea.

He'd label that Phase Four.

***

Mahan rapped on the door and heard Rose ask, "Who's there?"

"Just me."

The double locks snapped open and she let him in. As Mahan passed, he saw she had the stubby Colt Detective Special in her right hand, tucked behind her thigh. She'd brought it in after their session at the makeshift shooting range and never strayed too far from it while they were in the cabin.

"Staying sharp," he said. "That's good."

"It needs to be a habit, I expect."

"And you'd be right. Like second nature while you need it. After that…"

She closed and locked the door behind him. Mahan watched and said, "I'm going right back out again."

"Just you?"

"This time."

"How come?"

"Somebody called and left a message with the manager."

"That guy."

"Remember when I phoned to Kansas City earlier?"

Rose nodded. Didn't speak.

"I gave this contact number to the man I spoke with back there, earlier."

"That Mr. Pollard."

"Right. Asked him to pass on anything he might hear from his people in the field, regarding Simon Cain."

"Not thinking anything would come of it."

"Guess I was wrong."

"He called you here while we were out?"

"Not him." Mahan produced the desk clerk's note from his breast pocket, handing it to Rose. Watched while she read it through.

"Who's Archer Blake?"

"Beats me," Mahan replied. "Somebody from the Drought Relief Service, apparently."

"I see the 'DRS' that creep wrote down."

"According to the clerk—"

173

"The jerk," she interrupted him.

"Yeah, him. The caller claimed that Pollard got in touch with him, phoning around to his employees like I'd asked him to. This Blake ran into Cain a little while ago, and Pollard palmed it off on him to call me."

"So, why wouldn't he come here instead of setting up a meeting at...what's this address?"

"Clerk says it's an access road off Highway 40, back a mile or so and south of town."

"The middle of nowhere."

"My guess would be that Pollard said something to Blake about what Cain may have been up to lately. It makes sense for Blake to take precautions, getting in between a killer and a lawman, which he takes me for."

Rose frowned. "I want to come with you."

"That's not the best idea you ever had," Mahan replied.

"If there's no danger—"

"Nothing's set in stone. You're better off right here."

"Unless the jerk decides to stop by."

"I don't think he's smart enough to set this up."

"But he might try to take advantage of it."

"If he knocks, don't open up."

"He's got a passkey."

"And you've got your little friend." He nodded toward the Colt, still in her hand. "One look at that, he'll change his mind, and when I get back here I'll beat the shit out of him. If you haven't shot him first, that is."

"Promise?"

"And hope to die."

"Don't say that. It's not funny."

"No. Sorry."

"How long should this meeting take?"

"You see Blake didn't give a time. The clerk thinks that he called in about half an hour ago. I'll leave now, then I need to find the spot. From there, it all depends on what he has to say."

"And you'll be careful." Not a question; a demand.

"Sure thing."

"Because I know it's *not* your middle name."

"But words to live by, though."

"Remember that, will you? Both of our lives depend on it."

Trying to reassure her, Mahan said, "I should be back within an hour, ninety minutes tops. If Blake starts rambling on, I'll bring him back here with me."

"Better yet. Then we can both point guns at him."

"Maybe we should've passed on watching *Annie Oakley*."

"Jokes. Just what I need."

"Sorry again. I'll take off now. Sooner I go—"

"The sooner you'll be back."

"Exactly. Lock up after me."

"I'm not forgetting that. You've got the Magnum?"

"Yes, ma'am."

"Next time we go shooting, I might want to try out that one."

"It's a date," he said, and waited while she cleared the locks, then stood and listened while she fastened them again from the inside.

***

Simon Cain considered his next move. He estimated that he had a clear hour, approximately, while Mahan drove to the designated meeting place, found no one there, waited around for what would seem a decent interval, then realized he'd been deceived and doubled back to check on his companion at the Sunflower.

If Cain moved with dispatch, an hour was enough.

The clerk first, in case anything went wrong involving noise and prompted him to telephone police. Cain parked his Packard Twelve outside the tourist court's office and went inside, the trench knife riding on his left hip in its metal scabbard.

Putting on a smile, he raised a hand in greeting to the registration clerk, began to ask about a vacancy, then lunged across the counter, tangled fingers in his startled adversary's greasy hair and yanked him forward, head twisted to make his throat an easy target for the Mark I's thrusting blade.

Hot blood spilled across his knife hand while the dying man thrashed like a grounded trout, then gave up struggling for his life, gagged on the gore escaping from him, and went limp. Cain shoved him backward, dropping out of sight from anyone outside unless they entered, then peered over toward his body sprawling on the blood-slick floor.

Cain walked around the counter, hunkered down to wipe his blade and wet hand on the corpse's shirt tail, checked his watch and found that the initial operation had consumed just ninety-four seconds.

Still ample time.

Returning to the Packard, Cain got in and moved it down the line of cabins to an empty space in front of number six. It would have been too obvious in front of number seven, but he needed it nearby in order to complete his exit strategy.

The hard part faced him now.

Her approached the door emblazoned with a dull brass digit "7," knocked lightly and waited for an answer from within. The girl should be inside, nowhere for her to go unless she made the trip on foot, and he assumed that she would not wish to expose herself, whoever she might be, whatever her connection to the Texas Ranger.

Cain would learn all that in time.

A muffled, worried-sounding voice came to him from beyond the cabin's door.

"Who's that?"

"You don't know me," he answered affably. "My name is Archer Blake."

A moment of predictable, uneasy silence followed that before she said, "You aren't supposed to be here."

"No, you're right," Cain said. "I'm trying to find Wallace Mahan."

Further anxious hesitation, then, "He's gone to meet you at the place you called about."

"Correct. He never showed, and since he had no way to phone me back, I thought…well, I don't know exactly *what* I thought, but it's important that I speak to him."

"He should be waiting there right now. You gave the manager directions."

"But he may have got them wrong," said Cain. "I just saw him. I have to say, he's not the brightest guy I ever met."

"You got that right."

"So, anyway, he sent me down here. Said to ask you. Maybe I could come inside and wait for Ranger Mahan?"

"No. You'll have to wait outside."

"Okay," he said. "Suits me all right, but I'm not sure about the manager, you know? He sees me standing here too long, he may get spooked and call the cops."

"Is that a problem?"

"Not for me, ma'am. I don't know about for you, the Ranger, or whatever."

She considered that, a silent moment passing, then she said, "I need some proof of who you are."

"Such as?"

"A driver's license, maybe, or your Drought Relief card."

Damn it!

"Sure," Cain said. "Okay. But I don't see a peephole in your door and there's no mail slot."

"Try to slide them underneath."

Cain glanced down, his patience wearing thin. Reminded her, "There's weather stripping."

"Guess you're out of luck, then."

Another pause, while Cain pretended to examine cabin number seven's door. "Hold on," he said. "Looks like it might be possible to slip my license through a crack above the dead bolt. Will you try to catch it?"

"Go ahead."

Cain gave the girl a second to move closer, bending forward, while he glanced to left and right. No living person in the office; no cars close on either side of his. He was as safe right now as he would ever be again.

Cain reared back, kicked the door with his right foot, as hard as he could manage. Locks shattered. The door flew inward, made a solid *thump* when it struck the young woman squarely in her face. He followed through and swung it shut again behind him, saw her sprawling on the floor, blood oozing from her nose.

And stopped dead when he saw the small revolver pointed at him, wavering in her unsteady hand, aim shifting from his face to groin and back again.

"Go on, then," Cain said, daring her. "Do it, if you think you can live with what comes next."

"I'll try my best," she said.

And fired.

***

Off Kansas Highway 83

Mahan was starting to believe he'd been stood up. It wouldn't be the first time that a meet with an informant fell through on him, but he couldn't think of any other instance that he'd cared about so much.

The access road to which he'd been directed by the note from Arthur Blake—maybe a pseudonym—was one-lane dirt and gravel south of Oakley, branching off to westward from the north-south run of Highway 83 that led to tiny Elkader and then Scott City, if he'd kept on driving far enough. The land surrounding him was gray and rippled like the ocean's surface, but with dust, not frothing waves. A rusty, sagging barbed wire fence followed the access road's south side.

And Mahan was alone.

He'd spotted tire tracks, pulling in, that told him someone in a car *had* been there recently, drove in as far as he was now, then turned around and backtracked to the two-lane blacktop. He could see a mile or more toward any given compass point, and there was no one standing, sitting, even lying on his belly like a sniper in the bleak landscape.

Mahan shifted the Smith & Wesson in his belt, glanced at the watch on his left wrist, remembering Rose's misgivings when he'd briefed her on the meeting. She'd suggested it might be a trick—a thought he'd naturally shared—but felt that it was worth the risk. Mahan had survived a few ambushes in his time and walked away, while those who'd meant him harm did not.

Now, standing alone with no trap closing on him, Mahan wondered if this Blake, or whatever his name was, might have chickened out, deciding it was better all-around if he just disappeared instead of showing up. There was a precedent for that, as well.

Starting to fume, he gave the man he'd never met ten minutes more, then cursed him for a coward as he got back in the Model A, reversing through the wasteland. Driving back to Highway 40 and the Sunflower, he planned to have a word with Billy Goat, the manager, after he'd checked with Rose and told her she'd been right, the contact fizzling out.

Tomorrow morning, when the feds in Kansas City started taking calls, he would be on the line to Jacob Pollard, trying to make sense of the mix-up.

As Mahan pulled into the Sunflower's parking lot, he glanced in through the office windows and so no one. Never mind. That wouldn't stop him from confronting the Goatee and pressing him for further details on the call from "Blake."

He parked in front of cabin number seven and immediately noticed that its door was standing slightly open, no more than a couple inches, but the sight of it sent panic lancing through his chest. Pulling the Magnum without any thought of who might see it, Mahan bolted from the Ford and rushed to cross the cabin's threshold, shouting, "Rose!"

No answer, but it only took a heartbeat for him to discover what had happened. Someone had burst in upon her and there'd been a struggle. More, there'd been at least one gunshot fired. Mahan could still smell cordite in the cabin's one-room living area. Blood on the short-pile carpet told him someone had been injured, but he couldn't eyeball blood types and had no idea what Rose's was, in any case.

There were *two* spots where crimson stained the carpet, one stain larger than the other, but he couldn't say what that meant, either. Rushing to the little bathroom, just in case, he checked and found it empty, scowling at his own reflection in the mirror.

"Shit!"

Backtracking toward the open door, Mahan glanced to his left and saw a piece of paper resting on the pillow of the bed he'd occupied since they checked in the second time. He crossed to it, forgot all about fingerprints and such, lifting it close enough to read.

***

Ranger—

Your girlfriend did her best. You should have trained her better, but she'll make a decent sacrifice unless you're feeling like a hero.

Will you be her Savior?

***

It was unsigned, but he didn't need the author's name. Below the taunting message, more directions had been penciled in.

Another meet, this one where Mahan figured that he would not be left alone and feeling foolish.

Where the man he had been hunting now expected him to die.

Mahan could only guess at how much time had passed since Rose was taken, never mind how badly she was injured. If the kidnapper had killed her, Mahan reckoned that he would have left her in the cabin, maybe cut to pieces, and revised the content of his note.

Oppressed by passing time, Mahan still had one further job to do before he left the Sunflower and sought directions to the killer's chosen place of execution. Jogging to the office, he went in, shouting for service, then saw blood smeared on the surface of the registration counter. Looking over, he saw Goatee, throat gashed, bled white.

Knife work. No answers there.

Mahan left someone else to find the stiff and call police. He had no further time to waste. He stopped once more, the first gas station that he came across, and tried to keep from yelling at the pump jockey while asking for directions. Tipped the kid a dollar, nodded at his mumbled thanks, and drove off toward the showdown he'd been waiting for.

Was he too late for Rose? If not, how could he help her best?

For that, he'd have to scope the ground, then make a plan.

Whatever else happened, the hunt was ending now. Today.

17

The flesh wound in Cain's side, above his left hip, throbbed with pain but he had bandaged it to stanch the bleeding. He was lucky that the girl had never shot a man before and couldn't stop her hand from trembling when she fired the only shot that he'd permitted her.

Her gun, a little .38, was lying on the seat beside him now, next to Cain's .45. He'd almost shot her in the cabin but controlled himself with iron will and a helping hand from God, disarming her instead and clubbing her unconscious with the Army automatic. Slender rope from one of his coat pockets bound her wrists and ankles before Cain saw to his wound, then penciled out his note to Wallace Mahan.

Driving, Cain had Fred Astaire on his car's radio, singing his U.S. Billboard number one hit "Cheek to Cheek." It was a jaunty tune and helped to cover up the sounds of Mahan's girl after she woke up, lying on the Packard Twelve's floorboard in back.

Cain didn't know her name yet, or what she was doing with the Ranger. There'd been no time for a round of twenty questions at the tourist court, but he would get around to that in time, once they had reached the killing ground and he'd prepared a proper greeting for their missing guest.

The spot he'd chosen was a long-abandoned farm, his kind of place, located two miles east of Oakley and a mile due south of Highway 40. Sharp eyes could spot it from the highway, but those passing wouldn't know the property was now deserted unless they investigated for themselves.

Cain had.

When he reached the spread, Cain pulled around behind its old ramshackle barn, gaps showing in the tin roof, angled toward the small farmhouse whose broken windows stared like dead eyes over nothing much. He left the girl squirming and sweating in the car, walking around to key the Packard's trunk and dress himself for battle, head to toe.

When he was satisfied with that, Cain buckled on his pistol belt, then lifted out his rifles, one by one. He checked the Enfield's load, then fixed its bayonet and slipped into a bandoleer of five-round stripper clips before he slung the rifle over his left shoulder on its leather sling.

Next out, the BAR, with two more bandoleers dangling. Cain walked it to the barn's wide-open double doors in front, facing the road, and leaned it up against the jamb, then set the bandoleers beside it, coiled like sleeping snakes.

He thought about grenades, still waiting for him in the Packard's trunk, but then decided they might be too much. Even out here, surrounded by nothing and no one, Cain considered that they might make too much noise, drawing attention from the highway, passersby driving with windows down, who would be curious enough to call police.

Gunfire, conversely, would seem normal on the open, empty plains, if it were even noticed.

His respiration quickened, hissing through the gas mask strapped over his face and head beneath the helmet, rasping in his ears despite the cotton wadded in them. He was ready to confront his enemy, perform the necessary sacrifice.

And after that, perhaps, the End of Days.

***

Rose strained against the bonds that held her hands behind her back and kept her ankles hobbled. She ignored the throbbing from her bruised face and the nose she feared was broken, sublimating pain, focused on her determination to survive.

She'd flubbed her one shot at the man who'd kidnapped her and cursed herself for that, listening as he rooted in the car's trunk, took his time about it, moving off and coming back again for reasons she could only work out vaguely in her mind. Setting a trap for Mahan, obviously, but beyond that she had no idea where they were parked, or any details of what her abductor had in mind.

If she could somehow slip free of her bonds, then…what? She had no weapons other than her hands, feet, maybe teeth, and he'd already proven strong enough to overpower her, besides the fact that he was armed with a pistol. Or two now, if he'd brought hers with him from the tourist court.

Not only that, she realized.

If her kidnapper was the random murderer she'd tracked with Mahan—and he *must* be, otherwise the weird coincidence was staggering—that meant he also had at least two other firearms and the knife he'd used to mutilate her family, along with others over time. He'd used a .30-06 rifle to dispatch her parents and her brother, then some fully automatic weapon on the homeless caravan in Logan County.

Mahan, for his part, had the .357 Magnum, shotgun, lever-action Winchester and Tommy gun, but he could only use one weapon at a time and wouldn't know what he was up against, assuming he could even find the madman's killing ground.

If she'd been grabbed by Simon Cain, that brought to mind his combat record overseas, the medals he'd received for killing Germans in the trenches before he was shelled, gassed and evacuated stateside to recover. That had obviously failed, perhaps healing his wounded flesh, but leaving his demented mind untouched, untreated.

Against that military record, Mahan had his years in service to the Texas Rangers, had killed men himself, though likely nowhere near the number Cain had shot, stabbed, strangled or whatever on the Western Front. It would be tantamount to fielding Red Grange on the gridiron against high school football players from the junior varsity.

Except that in this game, both sides would grapple to the death, no penalties and no timeouts.

She heard the man returning, feigned unconsciousness but didn't fool him as he drew open the Packard's left-rear door, leaned in and slapped her hard enough to make Rose cry out in surprise. Immediately afterward, he pressed the muzzle of his automatic to her temple, bearing down on it.

"Don't even think of getting frisky," he commanded. "I'd prefer you to be breathing when he joins us, but you give me any grief and you can meet him when he catches up with you in Hell."

He grabbed the collar of her shirt and Rose heard fabric ripping as he dragged her roughly from the car to dump her on the ground. She stared up at him, vaguely recognized the gas mask he was wearing, and the other bits of military garb, feeling a chill race through her as her eyes confirmed what she'd already known.

The bastard was a raving lunatic.

"We're going over to the barn now," he informed her, cluing Rose in for the first time to the fact that they were on somebody's farm. The owners were apparently long gone, blown west by dust storms or trying to earn their keep from odd jobs, begging or whatever in a city where the cops were too lazy or overwhelmed to drive them out.

Rose found her voice. Told him, "I can't walk with my ankles tied like this."

"That's why I tied them," he informed her. "Just relax and let me do the work."

That said, he dragged her twenty feet or so, in through the open backdoor of a barn that seemed halfway toward falling over if another stiff wind came along. Musty inside, the smells of dust and mold combined, and muggy even with the doors opened to front and back.

He left her near the broad front doors, lying on her left side, facing a desolate barnyard, a broken-down corral, and part of a dilapidated farmhouse. Said, "You ought to have a fair view of the show from here, when your boyfriend shows up. Make any noise, and when I'm done with him, you'll get a taste of bayonet practice. Nod if you understand me."

Rose nodded, fighting back angry tears.

***

Mahan spotted the farm buildings when he was still the better part of two miles out. At that range, he could see no signs of human habitation, calculating that the former tenants had evacuated, but he wasn't taking any chances as the purple shades of dusk came on.

Before he needed lights to drive by, Mahan pulled over and switched off the Ford's engine, opened its driver's door and stepped out, stretching as he stood beside. The Model A had no dome light that came on automatically, like certain more expensive vehicles now, so he was safe on that score. Khaki-clad and shielded by his dusty auto, flanked by miles of nothing as the night came on, he was as sheltered as he'd ever be from whoever was waiting for him on the played-out farm.

Was Rose there? Was she still alive?

He knew of only one way to find out.

Mahan lifted the Model A's backseat cushion and started hauling out his arsenal. The rifle and his shotgun both had shoulder straps for carrying, which left his hands free for the Tommy gun. He checked each weapon's load, slotted the Tommy's hundred-round drum into its receiver from the left, after he'd manually wound its tension spring.

Inside the drum were six compartments that rotated as the weapon fired. Four slots held twenty cartridges apiece, the last two packed with ten each. With the fifty-round drums there were still six sections, four of ten rounds each, the other two with five apiece. Once he had snapped the drum in place, Mahan drew back the Thompson's cocking lever, set on top of its receiver, made for firing from an open bolt.

Four guns, loaded with 125 rounds of ammunition, including one each in the chambers of his rifle and shotgun besides the ammo in their magazines. Then multiply six shotgun rounds by nine pellets of double-aught buckshot apiece. Call it 173 projectiles without reloading, and Mahan could have killed an army company with that, except that they—and his opponent on the farm—would all be shooting back, trying to take him down.

He had a slim advantage, knowing part of what his enemy was armed with from crime scene ballistics evidence, but there could still be more surprises waiting for him and he wasn't pleased about the prospect of grenades. The killer's Enfield and his BAR, both firing aught-six rounds, surpassed the range of any weapon Mahan carried. His Smith & Wesson Model 27 came the closest, firing Magnum rounds, but accuracy faded in the stretch thanks to its 3.5-inch barrel.

Never mind.

He knew what killing was, what it entailed, and he was motivated by the knowledge that if he failed, if he died, it also meant death for Rose Halliday.

"Not on my watch," he warned the night, but it rang hollow in his ears.

***

Cain sat above the farmyard, in the barn's hayloft. Climbing its ladder had been risky, one rung giving out on him, but he had persevered and found the second-story flooring fairly solid once he got that far.

Seated with legs crossed on a bed of moldy hay, the Enfield in his lap, Cain scanned the battlefield in front of him as light drained from the sky. He had not sighted Mahan yet, no headlights on the access road, and had begun to wonder if the man who had been stalking him would find the place or even try.

It seemed unlikely that the Texas Ranger would abandon his young traveling companion, but experience had taught Cain that the only thing one person could predict about another was that he or she might wind up being unpredictable. Lawmen learned certain tricks if they were going to survive, as soldiers did, and while the army's brass spoke endlessly of honor, code and duty, Cain knew cops were often underhanded and duplicitous. Even the ones who didn't steal might still lie under oath to make a case, and some were willing to entrap or frame a suspect if they came up short on evidence.

If all else failed, a gunshot fired in "self-defense," supported by a throwdown knife or gun, would send a reprobate to his reward.

"But not this time," Cain muttered to the night.

And when he'd dealt with Wallace Mahan, he would make the girl tied up below him scream for hours.

By the time he finished with her, death would come as sweet relief.

A subtle movement on the darkling field in front of Cain focused his full attention on the spot. It might be nothing, or…

No! There it was again, most certainly a man this time, trying for stealth as he approached the farm. He moved in fits and starts, a few yards at a time, then froze, expecting cover from the shadows.

Too late.

Cain lifted the Enfield to his shoulder, thumbed the safety switch into firing position, and peered down range from the sliding ramp rear sight. His index finger slipped inside the Enfield's trigger guard and slowly started taking up the slack, a hair's-breadth at a time.

***

Rose felt the cord around her left wrist loosen, not enough to free her hand, but it was still encouraging. At first, she froze, glanced upward toward the hayloft as if her abductor might have heard the knot chafing at her abraded skin, but she knew that was ludicrous.

Instead of giving up, she redoubled her efforts, twisting first one hand and then the other, even welcoming a bloody seepage from her wrists if it would lubricate the cords and cause their grip to fail. She held her breath and strained, wriggled to back herself against the rough door jamb and let it work against her bonds.

How long until she could release one hand, and then the other?

As if answering her silent thought, a shot rang out above her, echoing inside the empty barn as if someone had dropped a firecracker into an oil drum. Shocked, she squealed aloud, then bit her lower lip, praying that her abductor had not heard.

No problem there.

He was too busy trying to kill Mahan.

Rose was almost ready for the second rifle shot, familiar to her from the gunfire that had massacred her family while she was looking for a place to hide and save herself. Through tears of fury, she stared off into the night but could see nothing of the figure coming under fire until another weapon answered there, its muzzle flash a yellow wink in outer darkness. Its report seemed muffled by comparison to her kidnapper's fire, a smaller caliber.

Mahan's Winchester, meaning he was still alive and fighting back. At the same time, she knew, he'd signaled his position and a third shot from the hayloft followed instantly. No answer came back from the Ranger's weapon and she swallowed back a sob, afraid that he'd been hit that time.

If so, he might still be alive, but—

"*No!*" Rose hissed between clenched teeth, flexing her arms and shoulders once again.

And suddenly she felt her left hand slither free.

The right hand followed almost instantly. Rose bent to grapple with the knots around her ankles while a fourth shot from the hayloft made her jump.

What was the madman's target now?

Freeing her legs required another moment, then she rose, trembling from having been immobilized so long, and scurried toward the far side of the open double doors, where her tormentor's Browning Automatic Rifle leaned against the other jamb.

Rose clutched the weapon, picked it up, and grimaced at its weight, the better part of twenty pounds. She'd never held a gun so heavy in her life and realized she had no clue about its operation, how to cock and fire it, much less whether she could aim and hold it steady if she managed that.

The only thing Rose knew was that she had to try or die in the attempt.

***

The first shot nearly parted Mahan's hair. It might have if he hadn't worn his hat, after considering whether to leave it in the Ford and then deciding what the hell.

The aught-six slug punched through the crown of Mahan's Stetson—the cattleman's style, not the Boss of the Plains—and sent it flying off into the night. Another inch or so lower, and maybe if he'd left the hat behind to give his enemy a better target, he'd have been stone dead, his brains mingled with boot prints in the dust.

But as it was, he lived, ducked low and dodged off to his left before the second rifle shot came rattling by him like a Lilliputian freight train. Mahan hit the deck, cradling the Tommy gun, the two Winchesters on their shoulder slings first pummeling, then gouging at his back. It hurt both ways, but nowhere near as bad as being shot.

He'd glimpsed the sniper's first shot, from its winking muzzle flash, but missed the second as he ducked to save himself. The third, from Mahan's prone perspective, seemed to come from well above ground level, call it fifteen, twenty feet or so.

Trees were in short supply out here, so scratch that possibility. Which meant the shooter must have found himself a stable manmade platform, say a roof or something similar— or on a farm, perhaps the open hayloft of a barn.

Setting his Thompson to one side, Mahan unslung the Model 1892 Winchester rifle, shouldered it and thumbed its hammer back, waiting until the sniper tried again. It didn't take him long, no more than half a minute, but he hadn't found his mark and Mahan squeezed off from his belly-down position, then rolled to his left, in case his adversary spotted where he lay.

A good thing, too, since when the next aught-six round rattled in, it raised a spurt of dust approximately where he'd been stretched out a moment earlier. Mahan returned fire, rolled again, and his opponent scored another miss.

That could go on all night, he realized, with only dumb luck finally deciding who won out. Meanwhile, he didn't have a clue where Rose was, whether she was even still alive, and Mahan didn't feel like wasting any further time.

He wriggled back into the lever-action rifle's sling, rose

to a crouch, and grabbed his Tommy gun. Advancing in a zigzag pattern, he began to close the gap between himself and whoever was bent on killing him.

He had the man who'd murdered Nora and her family almost within his grasp.

Mahan just wished he had a notion who in Hell that was.

***

Simon Cain cursed, then caught himself, and hissed a quick apology to God through his gas mask. Somewhere below him and within a hundred yards or so, a mortal enemy was closing in and Cain had no idea precisely where he was.

Biting his tongue to keep from spewing more profanity, he drew the Enfield's bolt back, plucked one of the stripper clips from his infantry-issue bandoleer, and slid five rounds into the rifle's open breech. Closing the bolt chambered one .30-06 cartridge, leaving four more still in the weapon's magazine.

He thought about the BAR waiting downstairs, decided maybe it would serve him better in his present circumstance. With that, he could lay down a sweeping stream of fire and have a better chance of leveling his prey, even without a clear-cut target in his sights.

Rising, Cain started toward the hayloft's ladder, moving in a crouch, when suddenly Unholy Hell erupted all around him. It began with automatic weapon's fire from outside, bullets chewing through the second-story barn walls, spraying him with wooden splinters and hot shards of lead. He couldn't judge the weapon's caliber, although he had a hunch, and from its rate of fire suspected it must be one of the Thompson submachine guns he had coveted without so far acquiring one.

Almost before that thought had registered, more automatic fire—closer and louder—rattled from *below* him, heavy bullets punching through the hayloft's wooden floor, a couple of them nipping at the hem of Cain's greatcoat, one ricocheting off the metal scabbard of his trench knife.

He was spewing curses, no time to request forgiveness from his Savior, when the floor dropped out from under him and Cain plunged into freefall.

Impact with the barn's dirt floor shot stabs of pain up through his left ankle and knee, into the hip. He fell in that direction, landing heavily, and lost the Enfield somewhere, right hand groping for his pistol in its flap holster.

And as he reached the automatic, drew it, cocked it with his thumb, dazed eyes reported to his brain a shocking sight.

The girl, still nameless to him, knelt before Cain with the BAR in hand, its muzzle drooping. She had managed to untie herself somehow, had seized the unfamiliar weapon and unleashed the better part of half a magazine to bring him crashing down from the hayloft. It was a miracle she hadn't disemboweled him in the process, and Cain seized on that—his Father's blessing—as he raised the Colt to fire.

Their guns went off together, her rounds from his weapon tearing up the barn floor, raising clouds of dust between them like a smokescreen, Cain's two shots recoiling in his fist. He saw her tumbling over backward, with the Browning's last rounds jolting it out of her grasp.

She landed on her back, squirming, as Cain rose to his feet. That took a moment, fighting through the pain on his left side, but then he made it, sighting down the Colt's slide at the female who had very nearly killed him.

He was on the verge of firing, a split-second from it, when

a man's voice from the barn's broad doorway said, "You look fucking ridiculous."

***

At first, Mahan couldn't believe his eyes, seeing a tallish man dressed like a doughboy from the war in France, from helmet down to combat boots, the gas mask on his face giving the aspect of a praying mantis grown to human size. But once he took it in, he thought, *Why not?*

Wouldn't a raving lunatic dress up like one?

His words surprised the gunman, made him turn away from Rose, bringing the .45 to bear on Mahan. From inside the mask, he wheezed, "I hoped that you'd be here to watch her die."

"Not happening," Mahan replied, his finger tensing on the Tommy gun's trigger.

The make-believe soldier got off one shot, the bullet biting deeply into Mahan's left side, just above his belt. Falling, Mahan held down the Thompson's trigger, fought its recoil with a firm grasp on its pistol grips, both fore and aft. The awesome rate of fire emptied its drum in seconds, spitting out the final seventy or eighty .45 ACP rounds, his target jerking, dancing, reeling in a cloud of crimson spray.

The impact of collapsing to his knees propelled a grunt of pain from Mahan's lungs. He toppled over on his wounded side, the Thompson slipping from his hands, as he saw Rose lurch to her feet and rush in his direction.

He could see her lips moving, but words were out of synch, seeming to reach his ears a heartbeat later and from far away. His chest seized up and he was going, going, gone, barely aware that she was begging, "Hold on! Please don't die!"

18

Hays, Kansas

He didn't die. Oakley physicians stabilized Mahan, removed the bullet from his side, then sent him eighty-seven miles by ambulance to Hays, the largest city in northwestern Kansas, for continued treatment at the Ellis County Hospital. On his fourth morning there, after a bland and tepid breakfast, Rose came in to see him wearing clothes he hadn't seen before and looking none the worse for wear.

"They told me you were in the clear," he said, as she leaned in to kiss his stubbled cheek.

She raised the short sleeve of her floral-patterned blouse, left side, to show a bandage peeking out from underneath. "Just grazed me," she allowed. "You got the worst of it."

Mahan tried shrugging, winced and gave it up. "It's not the first time I've been shot."

"You need to watch that, what I've heard about your heart."

"Doctors exaggerate."

"A myocardial infarction's what they're calling it. That means a heart attack."

"I normally take pills," he said, feeling a little sheepish.

"And forgot to mention that."

"I didn't want to worry you."

"The staff here is supposed to keep police from nagging you."

"They're doing pretty well," Mahan replied.

Could have done better, though.

Not that he cared, since Nora and his grandson were avenged, Rose safe and sound.

When she had finished gently scolding him, Rose asked, "You're going back to Texas now, I guess."

"Guess so. Soon as they let me out of here."

"And mind your doctors down there, when they tell you to relax?"

"There's not much else for an old man like me to do."

"Old man, is it? You saved my life."

"Seems like the other way around, you and that BAR."

"It almost knocked me flat," she granted. "I'm still not sure how I got it working."

"Like a pro, from what I hear."

"Another Annie Oakley. Maybe I could join a Wild West show."

"I'd buy a ticket," Mahan said.

"On second thought, I'm not sure that's the real me."

"You've got time to work it out."

"I hear you've had some visitors."

"A few," Mahan agreed.

In fact, he'd counted thirteen sheriff's deputies and homicide detectives stopping by from various departments while he convalesced, asking how he "got onto" Simon Cain when their respective agencies had not. Mahan had referred them

to the telephone and leg work, leaving out his talk to Agent
Frank O'Neal in Dallas and the former DRS director Jacob
Pollard who, he understood, had dropped from sight and was
presumed to have been murdered by "persons unknown." That
was, unless you asked his ex-wife, who suspected he was off
somewhere living the high life with "some tramp" and screw-
ing both of them—the hussy just for fun, his ex for alimony
payments that had stopped when he dropped out of sight.

Mahan wasn't betting on that and felt a twinge of sorrow
for his part in getting Pollard killed, assuming Cain had done
the deed.

Captain Bolton from Motor Vehicle Inspections also made
the trip east from Topeka, glowering at Mahan in his bed and
saying he'd appreciate it if Mahan got out of Kansas when
the medics rated him as fit to travel. Mahan hadn't thought
about it, but professed a plan to do just that, then Bolton had
surprised him with a limp handshake before he left.

An agent from the FBI in Kansas City—the Missouri
one—had come to visit Mahan yesterday. His name was Pe-
ter Shaughnessy and he was red-faced, with receding hair,
a smattering of freckles, and he'd mostly talked about his
bureau's lack of jurisdiction in the murders Cain committed,
"if in fact they were connected." Overall, he'd looked embarrassed on his agency's behalf. He'd made no reference to
Mahan's conversations with Agent O'Neal and Mahan had
not felt the urge to bring it up. Before he left, the G-man told
Mahan, "You shouldn't try this kind of thing again."

He had no answer when Mahan replied, "Who else would
do it, then?"

The Rangers hadn't sent a man, but on his third day in

the hospital Mahan received a Hallmark get-well card from Austin, signed by the captain of his former troop. The card portrayed a bloodhound lounging on a porch beside a rocking chair. Below the captain's signature he'd penned, "Nice job. Ever consider coming back?"

Mahan had not, nor did he bother to respond.

Rose brought him back to then and there, saying, "So, you were right. It was Cain all along."

"Not me," Mahan reminded her. "The Texas FBI and Jacob Pollard from the DRS."

"Poor Mr. Pollard. I was sad to hear what happened to him."

"No one seems to know what happened."

"We do, don't we? It was Cain. It had to be."

"Nothing to do about it now, if that's the case."

"One of the cops I talked to claims the government has fired him, cutting off his pension."

"That will disappoint his former wife."

"It's rotten, though. Cain murdered him, and Mr. Pollard goes down in the record as a quitter who just up and left his job without a word to anyone, for no good reason."

"Did you try to talk them out of it?" he asked.

Rose blushed and shook her head. "I figured it was better just to say nothing at all."

"Good call. The less they feel a need to question you again, the better off you'll be."

"Speaking of that…"

"Go on."

"Well, um…I wondered where we might be headed next."

"We?"

"You know that I've got no kinfolk left," she said. "I can't go back to Lyon County, waitress in some diner if they still have one, with everybody staring at me, whispering behind my back or asking nosy questions to my face."

"That doesn't sound too good, I grant you."

"Are you heading back to Texas?"

"It's my home, or was, before all this."

"But maybe doesn't feel the same today?"

"I haven't given it a chance."

"Well, I was thinking…"

"What?"

Se hesitated, then said, "Since I've got no place to go and you aren't sure about where you'll wind up, couldn't we—"

"That's the second time you've used the 'we' word," Mahan interrupted.

"I just thought…"

"What do you figure folks would say, a damned old coot like me being with somebody your age who looks like you?"

Rose frowned at that. "What's wrong with how I look?"

"Not one damned thing, and you know it."

That perked her up a little, but she was relentless. "Who cares what some busybody says about a fellow and his niece?"

"We're still related, then?"

"Why not? If need be, we can get the records from Topeka that confirm it."

Mahan frowned. Said, "Any niece of mine would be in school."

"I beat you to it," Rose replied. "I graduated back in June, out of Emporia High School."

"And if your uncle was to ask your plans for whatever comes next?"

"I'd likely tell him that I take it one day at a time."

Mahan suppressed an urge to smile at that. Instead, he told her, "You should know the doctors say my problems won't be over when the hole Cain put in me has finished healing up."

"About your heart, you mean."

"That only ends one way."

"Same way we all do," Rose replied. "Look, I'm not angling for you to adopt me. Chances are I'll meet somebody, sometime, maybe settle down."

Mahan feigned shock and clutched his chest. "The hell you say! Who is this whippersnapper you've been sneaking off with while my back was turned?"

That made her laugh. And that, in turn, made Mahan feel a little better, even medicated as he was and still in pain.

"We'd have to play it cagey," he said, as the moment passed. "Make sure to keep our stories straight."

"No problem there. I figure us for master-minds."

"You know what preachers say about the sin of pride?"

"I might have heard it once or twice. You want to, we could join a church somewhere. Cover out tracks."

"Let's not get too carried away," Mahan advised. "I've had enough of preachers for a good long while."

"So, are we trying it?"

"Well…"

"Can I call you 'Uncle Wally' now?"

He pulled a frown at that and said, "Don't push it, kid."

ABOUT THE AUTHOR

A California native, Michael Newton has published 215 books under his own name and various pseudonyms since 1977. He began writing professionally as a "ghost" for author Don Pendleton on the best-selling Executioner series and continues his work on that series today. With 104 episodes published to date, Newton has nearly tripled the number of Mack Bolan novels completed by creator Pendleton himself.

Newton's first book under his own name was Monsters, Mysteries and Man (1979), a survey of unexplained phenomena for younger readers. While 156 of Newton's published books have been novels—including westerns, political thrillers and psychological suspense—he is best known for nonfiction, primarily true crime and reference books.

SKINWALKER:
A GIDEON THORN WESTERN HORROR OMNIBUS

MICHAEL NEWTON HAS WHIPPED UP A COLLECTION OF CHILLING TALES THAT WILL LEAVE YOU BREATHLESS.

Gideon Thorn, survivor at age two of the unknown 'animal' attack that massacred his family in Kansas Territory, roams the West in search of answers to his personal tragedy and other unsolved mysteries of seeming paranormal origin.

Gideon confronts his early fear—perhaps his very fate—on hallowed ground… he must now face an unworldly threat from one dispossessed of what was rightfully his…and there's no greater foe, man, or beast.

Follow Gideon Thorn as he investigates the unknown that could lead him to the very mouth of Hell.

Skinwalker: A Gideon Thorn Western Horror Omnibus includes – Skinwalker, Leviathan Rising, Ghost Town, Mountain Devils, Soul Slayers, Hallowed Ground, Night Flyers and Empty Graves.

AVAILABLE NOW